RECLAIMING JOY

Cover Art by Maria Spada

https://www.mariaspada.com/

RECLAIMING JOY

A WRITEHIVE ANTHOLOGY

KIERA ALVENTOSA   R. JEAN MATHIEU

CARTER LAPPIN   EMMA SLOLEY   RAVEN J. DEMERS

S.M. FOX   EMMERYN PALLADINO   VALERIE HUNTER

K.M. VEOHONGS   KARL EL-KOURA

LINDSAY MANSFIELD   MATT BLISS   SARINA DORIE

ARWEN SPICER

Edited by
JUSTINE MANZANO
Edited by
DAKOTA RAYNE

CONTENTS

FOREWORD

Reclaiming Joy is the second book in our anthology. In *Navigating Ruins*, our stories focused on how to cope after drastic, life-altering change. But when we emerge on the other side of the ruins, it's time to rebuild not just hope, but our inner peace.

Many times what brought us happiness no longer exists, or it has been irrevocably changed. There's a journey, a process that happens where we struggle to find the positive when everything seems dismal and dark and endless. *Reclaiming Joy* is not just for others, but for ourselves. The tiniest shred of happiness can change our perspectives, keep us going for another day.

The stories of finding and treasuring these moments in our lives are as powerful and vital as those of enduring tragedy. They remind us of the good in the world, of hope that is buried underneath difficult times. There's so much beyond our control within the world, but we can claim pieces of joy for ourselves, and there's a power in that.

Within this anthology, the authors explore the reclamation of wonder and self-worth. Some are light-hearted tales, while others explore joy after tragedy or fear. Each story is a unique perspective. We hope you enjoy the collection and find inspiration to reclaim joy in your own life.

Bee the Change,

Jerusha René (she/her)
WriteHive CEO

BEFORE THE BLOOM

KIERA ALVENTOSA

The first time we stole, I was seven. My grandma, Yaya, dressed me up in my nicest clothes, a dark blue dress with a lace collar, and shiny black shoes. She picked up her purse.

"Are we going to church without Mommy and Daddy?"

"No, cariño." She straightened the bow on my dress. "You just follow Yaya, okay?"

We walked in the summer heat until I was sticky with sweat and itchy in my dress. My buckled shoes pinched my toes with every step. I didn't complain.

We were on the other side of town, where the buildings were tall and made of glass. We walked through the sliding doors of the grocery store. The bright light hurt my eyes as I trailed behind Yaya. I tucked my arms into my dress against the cool blast of the refrigerated section and stared at the food.

The shelves were fully stocked. Fruit, vegetables, bread, and pastas of all shapes and sizes.

Yaya raised her chin the way she always did, sure of herself, and walked through the aisles. She grabbed a bag of apples and then another. We walked to an empty corner, blocked from view by the cereal section. She tore open the bag and emptied it into her purse. She shoved a bag of rice on top. I knew not to say anything when she zipped her purse shut.

We paid for a pack of gum. I held her hand when we left the store.

Back then, I thought The Government couldn't have known how bad the shortages were. I thought they couldn't have known how we lived. But as I grew older, I knew that the center of the city was the place where food was concentrated, like a body retracting the blood from its limbs.

The part of the city where we lived, well, we were the limbs.

After a while, my grandmother stopped coming with me on shopping day. The walk into the center was too far for her and I knew her tricks by heart anyway. I gave up dressing nice too. I wore my jeans, and my hair was dirty. Even standing out the way I did, I knew I wouldn't be caught.

The sun was hot that day. Too hot even for June. Light bounced off the buildings and I squinted up at the roofs as I waited to cross the street. I tried to see the tops of the buildings.

My dad told me what it felt like to stand on top of a glass skyscraper. He was one of the many workers who labored under the sun, to harness the sun during The Great Transition. I remember how nervous my mom was back then. I swear all she thought about was him on that roof, and if he would fall off during installation.

Back then The Government's vision had been obvious. Solar panels to make the microgrids. Reduction of expenditure, energy efficiency, resilience in the face of natural disaster. I had to give them credit — this part of the city was stunning. Green leaves stood out against skyscrapers. The buildings sprouted plants from their sides, siphoning carbon dioxide from the air. The urban ecosystem was alive. The Government cared about how things looked on the outside.

I walked through the sliding doors. Ten years later and the cool blast of air at the entrance still dried the sweat on my forehead. I smiled and nodded at the security guard who stood by the entrance.

I squinted at his name tag. "Hey Chuck."

He frowned at me.

I strolled into the store, listening to the sounds of a woman as she argued with the cashier about her coupons. I scoffed, looking at her shopping cart. She should see our grocery stores. In The Bricks, we had limits on how many cartons of eggs a person could buy.

I picked up an empty basket someone had left in the aisle and walked like I owned the place. In my canvas bag, I felt my large metal water bottle bump against my leg.

Food prices had been high since the shortages started over ten years ago. Apparently, farms were under-producing because of another fungal blight. The Government had sent a few pamphlets explaining the issue and how there was "no further action that could be taken at this time."

All I knew was that we skipped dinner three times this week. If that didn't warrant this trip, I didn't know what would. I was light-headed but still thinking clearly. I barely needed to think anyway. I swung the bag by my leg and walked through the aisles. It was busy today.

My grandma and I usually mixed up the stores we would hit. I came here last week but it didn't matter. It felt good to be challenged. Security cameras in every corner, the security guard at the door. Come to think of it, surveillance had been increasing recently.

Yaya would cluck her tongue at me and say I was getting "too big for my britches," even though I told her that no one said britches anymore.

I kept walking, scanning the produce. I knew exactly where I was headed. The vegetable aisle was packed as usual. I grabbed our staples of onions, potatoes, and carrots. They were reduced cost for every bump and bruise. They wouldn't even know it was gone.

I moved to the cereals, pretending to read the label on a box of raisin bran. Yaya might want that to keep the bowels moving. I imagined the face she would make at me. Save it for the old people, she'd say.

As I stood there, contemplating her digestive tract, I used one of my sharp nails to cut into the bag of fingerling potatoes. I turned the corner and widened the opening on the bag. Then the baby onions. I put the basket on the ground pretending to stretch my shoulder.

The sign on the entryway wall read that shoplifting is a crime. "Thieves will face serious criminal penalties." That much was obvious. I had once seen a boy of around fifteen — my age — dragged out of one of these stores for trying to steal a box of pasta. The Government was not known for its leniency.

I finished the water in my bottle as a father and his son walked past me. Their shopping cart was full. Four containers of hot dogs, hamburger meat, and beer. For a summer barbecue most likely. The little boy wouldn't stop staring at me. I made a face at him. They should hire him for security.

I grinned as they rounded the corner. The aisle was clear. I was in the blind spot of the cameras. I poured the potatoes into my metal water bottle. I glanced behind me.

Clear.

I poured the small onions at an angle so they wouldn't bounce. I screwed the top of the bottle back on and stuffed the bags and their labels behind the oats. I left the basket on the floor.

I swung my canvas bag at my leg. Tonight, my family would have a proper meal.

I was nearly through the door when I saw it.

Chrysanthemum seeds. Mums. My mom's favorite because they were easy to keep alive. My dad had brought them home once for her. She admonished him for the expense, but I could tell she was pleased.

A few seeds couldn't hurt. I took a packet down.

I removed the barcode with my fingernail and slipped the

package up my sleeve. The packet of seeds shook like pebbles as I walked through the sliding doors.

Chuck stood on the other side. "I am just going to check your bag, ma'am."

I had learned to control my voice in moments like this.

"Yeah, sure. No problem." I opened the canvas for him. My right fingers clutched at my sleeve, pressing the packet of seeds to my wrist.

My metal water bottle was the only thing at the bottom of my bag.

"You were in there for a while. Didn't buy anything?"

I shrugged. "Didn't have what I was looking for."

He paused for a beat, before stepping back.

I began to walk away. "Have a nice day!" I tossed over my shoulder. That was too close. I wouldn't come back to this grocery store for a long time.

I chopped the onions for dinner. I tried to hide the tears that streamed down, knowing Yaya would make fun of me for being weaker than an onion.

My family would eat tonight. I was pleased with myself.

"Strips, not diced." My dad was helping my mom with the bills at the rickety table. The legs wobbled every time they went to write but he kept his eye on my dinner preparation.

We were making a Spanish tortilla. The moment I placed the potatoes and onions on the table, my parents decided on an early dinner. Yaya winked and patted me on the head. I didn't tell her about the seeds.

Yaya walked into the kitchen. "*Gracias a Dios*, we are starving," she said. "This damn *gobierno* doesn't care about us."

Mom looked up. I knew she would defend The Government. She always thought they were listening. As if they would bug our apartment, all the way across the city.

"Well, they can't control the blights. The fungus are resist —"

"Pah. Blights. Pah. What about the people?" Yaya lifted my arms into the air. "*Mira! Sus brazos!* Maria is too skinny. What about us?"

"Don't raise your voice," my dad said, always sure to defend Mom.

But Yaya had taken care of me when my parents were at work, and she would not stop now. To prove her point, Yaya wrapped her hand around my upper arm. Mom's eyebrows knit together in concern.

I pulled away gently, careful not to knock into Yaya. She was tinier than I was, with frail bones.

"I'm fine. I'm just growing."

Dad folded up some of the bills and patted Mom's hand. "We'll have to allocate more money for food then," he said.

Mom's knee bounced under the table. She nodded.

Dad plastered a smile on his face and stepped into the kitchen to help me. He took out his phone to play his favorite flamenco album.

"La fiesta va a comenzar . . ."

Dad lifted his arms, leaving the spatula in the pan, to clap beside his head. Mom smiled at him from across the room.

"Yo voy a pasar (pase usted) . . . Yo voy a pasar (pase usted) . . ."

When he started to stomp in time with the beat, we all joined in, laughing. He pulled my mom to her feet and began twirling her around the kitchen.

The scent of the tortilla flavored the air.

"*Ay que bo* — that's good," Yaya said.

The egg held the flavor of the potatoes and onion. The oils seeped together. I had two pieces even though I knew I should save one for tomorrow.

I was full for the first time in weeks.

The next night, I walked down to the corner of our street with the chrysanthemum seeds in my pocket. I didn't know when the flowers would bloom. All I knew was that when they did, my mom would smile again. That was enough for me.

The area around our apartment was energetic, vibrant, and a little run down. All of the culture that was lost in the structure and cold lines of The Glass Towers, lived here in The Bricks. It was overgrown and winding, streets paved and broken, but beautiful.

I looked across the way at my neighbors sitting on their stoop. They watched their children shriek with joy as they played on the sidewalk. This was a place to grow, to be alive.

It was home. The buildings sat lower and wider, so we could still see the sun rise and set each day. In the facing sun, I could see the shadow of the storm wall, which loomed over The Bricks as a constant reminder of the danger. The water was on the other side.

We would be the first to be swept away if the storm wall ever gave way, a fact we tried to forget. If the wall did collapse, The Government wouldn't have to worry about how many of us lived in The Bricks anymore.

I reached the empty plot of land on the corner of our street. After almost ten years of promised development, I knew without a doubt that it would be empty for a while still.

I knelt down in the dirt and pressed my finger into the ground. I poured the seeds into the holes and slowly folded the dirt over the top.

I knew it wasn't much, but it felt like something.

A few days later, I found a potato in the bottom of my canvas bag. I must have missed it the other night when we were cooking. The potato was sprouting, white roots growing in little shoots from every side.

Mom and Dad were at work. But Yaya was on the couch repairing my old jeans. "*Guapa*, what is that?"

I walked over to the couch to show her. "A potato and it's starting to sprout. *Mira*."

"*Ah, que bueno*. Let's put it in some water."

I shook my head. "Why?"

"It might grow."

I filled up an old plastic container with some water. I placed it underneath the window and waited.

I checked that little potato every day for two weeks as it grew in the corner of the room. We tried not to spill the water over the edges every time we walked by it.

And it grew — its bright green stalks standing straight with small root hairs growing from the base. At the top of the stalks, white flowers budded. I brushed my hand over the leaves.

"*Las patatas son grandes*. We should plant them somewhere with more space," Yaya said. "We are going to eat good in a couple of weeks."

I grinned at her. "I know a spot for it."

She looked at me and raised her eyebrow.

Yaya braided her long white hair back. I pulled on my sneakers, and she put on her slippers.

"*Vale*. Show me this place."

A knock on the door stopped us in our tracks. We didn't typically have visitors during the middle of the day in the summer.

Yaya shuffled over to the door. She didn't undo the chain lock, so the door only opened a crack.

"Who is it?"

"Open the door."

It was Mr. Derst, our landlord. My stomach dropped. Yaya straightened her apron and opened the door.

"Good morning," she said.

He looked past her, adjusting his navy suit. His hair was slicked back with oil. He looked around the apartment like he owned it, which he did, but also with a tinge of disdain.

I cleared my throat. "Ah, Mr. Derst, always a pleasure to see you."

"Don't be cheeky with me, girl." I nearly stuck my tongue out at him and his greasy hair. "I am doing some evaluations. This is my property after all."

He walked around our apartment, probably trying to fabricate damages.

Yaya moved to stand in front of our potatoes.

Mr. Derst pushed past her. "Well, what do we have here?" He reached down and picked up our beautiful flowering potato plants by their stems.

"This container could leak and cause permanent water damage." His eyes were beady. "This would violate your lease agreement."

I kept my body very still.

"It hasn't leaked. We are very careful, Mr. Derst. It is just a couple of flowers in water." Yaya looked taller than him, even in her slippers and apron.

"The contract you signed was clear. No growing plants in my apartment complex."

And with that he grabbed the potatoes by their stalks. He put them on the ground and proceeded to crush the white flowers beneath his black leather shoe. He ripped the stems from the base.

"Clean this up," he said.

Just like that. Our little hopes and weeks of growth had been crushed.

•　•　•

The door slammed, then silence.

Yaya grinned and moved her hands out from behind her apron. Clutched in her hands were three spudding potatoes, with their flowers intact.

"*Vale*. Show me the empty plot you mentioned."

I laughed hard, tears running from my eyes.

We looked down the hall to make sure the greasy bastard was gone. Then I led her down the stairs and out to the corner of the street.

I gestured to the ground. "I planted some mums here and they are beginning to push through the soil."

"Where did you get the seeds, *guapa*?" She was still using her pet names for me, so I knew she wasn't too angry about the whole big britches thing.

I put the potatoes down. "I, ah, found them. Outside the grocery store."

She gave me a long look. "Risky. Risky." She clucked her tongue once. "Next time get tomato seeds, *vale*?"

I chuckled and nodded. Always had her eyes on the prize, that one.

Yaya bent down on her knees and began digging into the soil with her bare hands.

The sun was hot overhead. The morning would have been a better time to start gardening. The dirt pressed uncomfortably underneath my fingernails, making them gritty and my hands dry. The hole was deep enough, and as we lowered the potato plant into the ground, we heard someone approach.

"Maria, Raquel, what are you doing?"

It was our neighbor from down the hall, Jacinta, with her kid.

Yaya beamed at her. "Planting these potatoes. Food is hard to come by these days, eh?"

Jacinta smoothed her son's hair back and nodded. "It really is. Did you ask Mr. Derst?"

At his name, Yaya's smile faded. She shrugged. "He won't notice for months. By then we should have some food."

Jacinta laughed. *"Es la verdad.* I'll come down and plant some basil then."

And so, the garden began.

It bloomed slowly. As our garden in The Bricks grew, our neighbors came to ask about the project. We learned together: about grafting, clipping, staking the weaker plants, weeding, flowering, and composting. Gerome and his family, who lived downstairs, brought a tomato plant the next week. We wove wire nets over the plants to keep the squirrels and rats out.

The first week, there was only one plot. The next week, Yaya had marked out a second. Our backs ached while we weeded the garden, but Yaya took this time to tell me stories. Yaya's father was a farmer of vegetables and fruit trees. She would tell her stories of the soil that our family's hands toiled in, pulling the potatoes from the roots.

On the day we finished planting our second plot, she called me over.

Yaya said, "As you know, my father, your great-grandfather, was a farmer."

I nodded.

Yaya hummed. "Your grandchildren will one day know that you were a farmer too."

The wind pushed through my hair. Yaya had a way of reminding me that the past and the future would always be woven together, sprouts and roots inseparable, both growing into and out of the soil.

A month later, we began to see the fruits of our labor. It was August and the tomatoes were ripening. They hung heavy on the stalks, but lavishly absorbed the sun. Their orange and red hues promised the flavors we could already smell. Its earthiness hung in the air.

We were connected and tied to this project. We planned out the division of food. The future vegetables we produced would be divided among the volunteers to take home. Yaya and I were beaming as we carried our two tomatoes home that night. We were proud of that little growth.

Later that week, we were finishing dinner when there was a knock on our door. No one moved to answer it. Knocking again, louder this time.

I dropped my fork. It clattered against the plate.

Yaya looked at me, concerned. Her eyes said it all. Mr. Derst. The garden. He must have found out. My thoughts raced. The security guard from the store. The cameras by the entrance. I pictured armed police officers at our door. All in black with two reflective stripes that ran down their uniforms.

My chest was tight.

My dad got up and walked to the door. He opened it mid-knock.

I stared at my plate. I didn't want to see the look on my dad's face when he realized what I had done.

"Ah, *hola, ¿cómo estás?*" His response was friendly, familiar.

"*Hola, muy bien, ¿y tú?*" It was a woman's voice.

I turned in my chair. Jacinta stood by the door. The breath I had been holding fled my lungs.

"Come in. Come in," Yaya said, waving her hand.

Jacinta was grinning as she stepped into our cramped apartment. She was clutching some papers and bursting with excitement.

"The land the garden is on. I found the owner."

Yaya turned her head. "I thought we decided that we weren't going to ask permission —"

Jacinta cut her off. "I got him to agree to let us use it for the next couple of seasons. *Mira*, he even signed this agreement I drew up."

Yaya and my mom stood up and rushed over to see the papers.

I leaned back against my chair and smiled.

I might always have these fears. The fear that one day The Government would find me. That one day our garden would be destroyed. That these little joys could be taken from me and from my community.

But in that moment, all I could think about were the flowers just starting to unfurl outside. The bees buzzing around them, pollinating our garden. The smell of the tomatoes hanging in the haze of the evening. Something small and seed-like pushed through to the surface, then bloomed.

ABOUT KIERA ALVENTOSA

Kiera Alventosa is a Hispanic American woman from Long Island, New York. In 2022, she received a MA in Writing from the University of Warwick, with a focus on environmental fiction, short stories, and poetry. This year, she completed a MSc in Nature, Society, and Environmental Governance at the University of Oxford. She can be contacted at kiera.alventosa@gmail.com or through her website, kieraalventosa.wixsite.com/kieraalventosa

THE VOLUNTOLDS OF AMERICA

R. JEAN MATHIEU

"The last time I saw Hope Hopkinson," Root says, "is when she hopped up on the tractor, nimble as a gazelle."

That's a lie. The last time she saw Hope Hopkinson was when Hope fell from the tractor, into the disc harrow. Root Bouziane watched Hope a lot. She'd been watching when Hope turned, a smile of bright teeth on a face dark as rich soil, to tell Archie Jeong a joke. That's when the tractor hit a stone. Root's scream had gurgled and died in her throat.

"The last time I talked to Hope Hopkinson," she continues, "we were joking about what she . . . what she'd call her garage. When she got out."

That's true, but misleading. Root had tried to interrupt Hope's notorious motormouth, to ask the question, to ask if there was room in her future for someone else. Someone like Root. She couldn't say it then, she couldn't say it now. She says something else instead.

"I mean, you remember how she'd go on and *on*." Root clears her throat. "'You guys, you *guys!* Computer science these days is all *performance art*. Okay? You do it to have *done* it, to pass the torch to the next code-monkey. The next code-monkey might even be you, okay? But the code? It's got a half-life like skittish Californium. I mean, if your code's there six months later, it's a tragedy. So I embrace it. You *gotta*. Never look back, right? You can't plot a trajectory from where you should've been, just from where you *are*. So change where you are, change the now, and you change where you can go — you change the future. Okay?'"

Melancholy laughter ripples around the circle. Apparently, she does a pretty good impression of Hope Hopkinson.

Twenty-two Voluntolds sit in the chicken coop that serves for housing as long as they're stuck here in Castroville, California, harvesting the world's artichokes. "Steinbeck country," as Root thinks of it. They're working a respectable heritage farm, certified genemod-free. The days begin before sunup and end after sundown, and the pesticides hang thick in the air.

When the artichokes are in, they will dutifully climb onto the recycled school bus emblazoned "Great Lakes Finance and Labor Solutions" and head north to pick grapes in Napa and trim the Humboldt marijuana harvest.

The chicken coop is drafty, especially with the foggy CalCoast autumn seeping in, but the wine-jug warms everyone. Hope would've wanted it that way.

"She was made of lightning," Root continues. "Like Walter said. So I joked she should call it 'Greased Lightning Garage.' And without cracking a smile, she turned to me and said *obviously* she'd have to call it 'Black Lightning Garage.'"

The laughter is louder this time, the kind of laughter that only comes from a black woman telling an off-color joke. Even if she isn't here to deliver it herself and it has to come through the cracking voice of a sad-eyed Lebanese girl from Connecticut. Root takes a deep breath, trying not to sob.

"I know we'll always remember her," Root lies. "I know we'll make her proud."

Her lies finished, she passes the talking-stick to Raymond Moretti and sips cheap wine.

"The last time *I* saw Hope Hopkinson," Ray says, "she was . .

. perky. Too perky for me. I mean, she was STEM, too — computer science, even. And she wound up in the Voluntolds like a fuckin' *English* major . . . er, no offense."

"None taken," says Root, coolly.

"Anyway. For the millionth time: 'Can't plot a trajectory from plotted position, only from current position.' And I said, c'mon, I studied electrical engineering, I *know* already. She peered at me, like this, and went 'do-o-o you?'"

The laughter this time is muted, half-aimed at Ray himself.

Root leans back in her creaky chair. The drafty chicken coop seems suddenly warm and stuffy, and not just because all twenty-two of them sleep on the floor together. Ray fades from her soundscape.

Hope Hopkinson had been part of the year's end-of-summer batch, with Ray and half a dozen others. Young, fresh, and full of hope — they still thought they'd serve their masters seven years, then finally be free to start off with nothing. Root knew better, but Hope and kids like her didn't irritate Root like they irritated grizzled vets like Walter. There was something endearing about them, something that made you want to hug them and kiss them. Especially Hope. Oh God, *especially* Hope . . .

Root groans to herself, her head sinking back. Her gold contacts detect null visuals as she gazes into the darkened rafters and pop up suggestions for local wines she might enjoy on her food-stamp stipend. She blinks the ad away, mutters "sleep." The vibrations travel up her jaw to her earband piercing, where the search engine hears all and obeys.

"I just can't believe it was *Hope*, of all people," Bonnie sobs.

"Would almost have to be the black girl," Walter Garcia mutters. "If only because of how overrepresented they are in this shitty program."

Root tries to listen to the work-gang's memories of Hope, but it's all in one ear and out the other. She *wants* to listen — this is the only commemoration Hope will ever get. But Root's brain swarms with despair. She's plotting trajectories.

After the circle is done and the talking-stick laid down, people cluster in twos and threes. Root just stands in the shadows, back against the drafty wall, sour new wine clutched to her chest. Already, Hope's memory is fading, evaporating in the night mists now that the circle is broken. There's living to do. Donald and Gary are already eye gazing, and svelte free runner, Bonnie, has her pick of Gerald or Karen. In six months, nobody will remember Hope Hopkinson. Nobody but Root.

The after-party is nothing Root wants any part of. So here she stands, chipped mug in hand, talking to herself.

Not to herself. To Hope.

"So what's *my* trajectory from here?" Root asks. "I drifted through high school and drifted into an English degree and drifted into the Voluntolds and I'm lucky as fuck I drifted into your orbit. But now you're gone. What's my trajectory? Orbiting the Voluntolds until I crash?"

She takes a gulp of sour wine, trying not to think of grain silos or choking pesticides or bloody disc harrows.

"I want *out*, Hope. I want to make art that people *actually pay for*, and I don't mean in fucking food stamps. So where can I go?"

She holds up a finger, glad everyone's too self-absorbed to notice her.

"I can pull a runner, like Wayne or Barb, but where'd they end up? The stupid-ass Voluntold red-white-and-blue stripes make everybody look like shitty flags, but they sure beat prison orange."

Another finger.

"I could enlist another seven-year term, but I'll be almost forty and who are we kidding? I'm not paying off an English degree from *Rutgers* in fourteen years. The stipends are balanced on state school fees, like your dear old *alma mater*, CSU Fullerton."

Another finger.

"Get a better job in the six months I got left? Doing what? I majored in English. So . . . barista? Maid? Bartender? Domestic? Didn't we go to college so that one day, maybe, we *wouldn't* be working minimum-wage service gigs? I couldn't pay off my loans in *forty* years on tips."

Her hand closes into a white-knuckled fist.

"Let's face it, all I'm good for is writing papers, drawing pictures, and picking oranges. God dammit, Hope!"

Root catches herself, bites her lip so hard that it bleeds.

"Sorry," she whispers, emptying her drink. She leaves the shadows to find the jug and pour another.

Root's hangover is so godawful, she can't stomach oatmeal. Fortunately for her, today is a holiday for Voluntolds Agriculture Corps #4077. They're heading into downtown Castroville to see a speaker. Hopping up onto the surplus-sale school bus, Root has flashbacks to high school assemblies and pep rallies. It beats back-breaking labor for sake of the world's artichokes, but still . . .

It doesn't help when the other kids start fighting.

"I'm just saying," says Curtiss, the AgSci major who made foreman by twenty-four. "If you look at *history*: Hillary. Rodham. Clinton. Got us into this mess."

Walter's customary scowl cuts deeper into his sun-seamed face.

"Are you claiming Hillary Clinton closed the borders, not President Robinson and all his Republican cronies?"

"How's that relevant?" Curtiss asks.

"The Voluntolds exist to fill a need," Walter insists. "First came Robinson's 'commonsense immigration.' Then, *all of a sudden, completely by surprise*, there's no ag workers, no construction workers, and a Second Great Depression."

"You can't blame Robinson for that, Walter!" Curtiss shakes his finger at the errant liberal on his work-team. "The Depression came after they voted in Lopez and the student loan bubble burst."

"Ahhh, yes," Walter mocks, "that weak-bellied, un-American Daniel Lopez. The one who solved the labor crisis with the loan crisis."

Everyone besides the debaters themselves groans. Curtiss has goaded Walter into lecture-mode, and now they would all suffer.

"In the finest possible way: the Voluntolds. A government-run, privately-operated corps of low-income labor. At fixed wages, of course, to help America's farmers and small businessmen. Can't cover education *and* rent? Volunteer to work for pennies, and we'll save dollars for you! Voila, the Voluntolds!"

Walter stands, offering himself as Exhibit A. Majored in Sociology, minored in Business. Spent the next twenty years trimming bud, picking grapes, and harvesting artichokes with the Voluntolds. Not going anywhere.

"You made my point for me, Walter," Curtiss says. "Lopez's liberals set up the Voluntolds, not the Republicans. Not Robinson."

"Lopez wouldn't've *needed* the Voluntolds if Robinson hadn't —"

"Jesus, guys, *shut up*," Bonnie says. "I'm trying to sleep."

Root looks out the window as they pull into downtown, her head pounding. On the side of the five-story Bank of America building next to the construction site, there's a mural. It shows a beautiful blonde who's been dead more than a century, the most famous begotten daughter of Castroville: Marilyn something, holding aloft cash-green artichokes and wearing a sash declaring her "ARTICHOKE QUEEN."

"Civic uglification project?" Ray sneers.

Everyone replies together: "Just life without arts majors."

No group lasts more than a month without in-jokes. Walter said that once.

Root keeps staring at the mural, at the garish blonde beauty queen. She pictures Hope Hopkinson there instead.

Hmmm . . .

Root smiles. It's the first time she's really smiled since Hope fell from the tractor.

They pull up to an Evangelical church that had once been Steinbeck Elementary. The fifty-something beaming from the pulpit looks like a telepreacher in a Voluntolds hoodie.

"Wilson Merchant!" he announces. "Voluntolds #3206, millionaire five times over, owner of six Trisolar service franchises across Northern California, member of the Monterey Chamber of Commerce, and a Rotarian. When my girls go to college, they'll each get a full ride from Dad, if they're careful."

He takes a deep breath.

"But, you know?" Wilson Merchant asks philosophically. "I'd trade it all to be back in the Voluntolds again."

Even Curtiss scoffs at this. Wilson Merchant holds up both hands. They are soft and lily-white.

"No no!" he says. "It's true! Those were the best years of my life, and I know they're yours, too. This camaraderie is something you'll never see again, the talking-circles and the night-runs games of MR Labyrinth. You don't have a care in the world. Heh! You don't even have to worry about your meals!"

He grins at them. "Unless you're on kitchen duty, of course."

It's at this point Root checks out. Most of the work-gang already have, their eyes glossing over in gold or silver, descending into mixed reality. But she sat next to Walter for a reason.

"What is this shit?" Walter grouses. "The powers that be want to cheer us up with a statistical erro — pardon me, *success story* — after Hope's reminder that we could die at any time thanks to their stringent safety standards."

"And what did Hope leave behind?" Root asks. "A few lines of code somewhere? Maybe her name on a paper? Some picked artichokes, a wake, and this pep rally from Hell. Well, *I'm* not gonna let her be forgotten. I'm going to leave a memorial to Hope Hopkinson that *nobody* will forget. Something past plucked artichokes and a few lines of code."

Walter is listening. She explains. She talks about the "civic uglification project." She talks about what farmhands look like now: Hope and Root and Walter himself.

She talks about a legacy.

When she's done, she stabs a finger into Walter's chest.

"And I'm gonna need your help," she says. "You were in Construction Corps before they transferred you to Ag, right?"

Walter nods. He'd been a welder until his hands started trembling. The wise actuaries at Great Lakes decided that picking oranges would be more his speed after that.

"You're gonna remember the girl made of lightning . . . in iron?" Walter says, his voice flat.

"Beats the shit out of standing to the side and complaining."

"You seemed happy enough last night," Walter says, clearly ruffled.

"I was *drunk*. Now I'm hungover and *still* doing more than you. What's stopping you? What are you afraid of?"

"Damages," Walter says. "I got two tours' paid-off loans to protect. *Ecce me*: self-interested American, Exhibit A."

"*Ecce tibi*, the eternal critic." That stings him. "We'll go anonymous. Like Banksy. C'mon. Do something for once."

Walter sighs. "Fine. Hope deserves better than Wilson Merchant boosterizing. Just . . . keep my name off it."

As they ride back to Hall & Sons on rickety bus seats, Walter and Root stare intently at the gaudy mural and at the construction site just next door.

It's when they pull up to the farm, back to reality, that Root's stomach falls out. She chews beans for twenty minutes, then trudges out through solar fields to the artichokes. Root's practiced hands move by themselves, her private soundscape swelling with rhythm. Even as the last vestiges of her hangover fade, Root remembers last night. God, had she *really* monologued like a Shakespeare villain at Hope? She must have been *so drunk*.

The clammy air flutters with ghosts of mixed reality, messages zipping back and forth or broadcast announcements or Curtiss' scoreboard logging who pulls the most 'choke heads — as if it means anything. Root watches numbers climb, and thinks about other numbers. Numbers that could change a woman's trajectory, break her out of orbit.

"But you'd *want* to change my trajectory, right, Hope?" Root answers for her: "Right."

Root ponders logistics, tosses another artichoke in the bin. She studied C! in high school, but to change her trajectory, she'll need more coding skills than that. Fine. She already needs a Modelo programmer to handle the MR side of the memorial. And she has just the kid in mind.

There he goes now, grabbing a drink of water under the tarp. Root joins him.

Many years ago, Root learned in psych class that there are two reasons anyone does anything: the *legitimate* reason and the *real* reason. The legitimate reason is the one you tell people at parties. But the real reason is what gets you out of bed in the morning. Usually a reason you never tell anyone.

Root has a legitimate reason for approaching Raymond Moretti. She needs a Modelo coder. That's the reason she'll tell Walter later.

"No can do," Ray says. "I got better things to do than wasting time on some fucking *art project*."

Root looks around. No one else feels like wasting their fifteen minutes on drinking when they might need to piss later. They're alone under the tarp. Ray is not Walter, he won't respond to ideals. He *will* set up backends . . . if properly motivated.

"It's not *just* an art project," Root mutters, *sotto voce*. "Thousands of people are gonna see it in person. Billions online. All those eyeballs . . ."

Ray's own eyeballs widen, wide enough Root can see the edges of his hi-tech contact lenses.

"The only real currency in the modern world," he quotes.

"Great Lakes Financial disagrees." Root swirls her water bottle and waits.

"So?"

"I'm hooking up a BQuest account for donations," Root says. "That's the easiest trajectory. There's data to sell and derivatives to harness . . "

Ray's eyes light up in a way that has nothing to do with Hanyin Optics.

"Frankly, it's too much for me to handle." Root waves off the phantom billions in Ray's eyes. "But I'm getting *out*, Ray. This isn't just an art project. This is changing my trajectory, settling my student loans once and for all. I need someone to manage the derivatives, someone in on the ground floor."

Ray nods, and takes a last swig from his canteen.

"Let's rap. But first . . ."

In unison, they say: "Fucking artichokes."

Each night after dinner, the three of them melt away from the stale jokes and petty vendettas and love affairs. In the barn, under hissing arc-light, Walter methodically assembles a handmade, iron-bound scancode. When it's finished, Walter's silver eyes and Root's golds will light up at first glance, quickening with visions and whispers of mixed reality.

Scancodes were printed on every conceivable product, on plaques next to museum exhibits and in out-of-the-way spots for ARG players to frolic. No one, to Root's knowledge, has printed one on nine square feet of galvanized steel in iron ingots and metal scrap.

Root's final design overlays the cold steel in spectral translucence, guiding Walter's flame. He works silently. She's tired of lying to him anyway.

Root works mostly with Ray, and not for the camaraderie. She writes and records content, bootstraps MR symbols they use to make new symbols. Root feels like a demiurge, forming the world with her words. Ray translates it into numbers, equations for the virtual world that overlays the physical like her design over-lays the steel plate.

She conjures a million Hopes out of thin air, from her dead media, from local news, from lens-recordings by Voluntolds of her smile and her laugh and her motormouth. Root spends hours with these ghosts, her eyes lingering on the curve of her cheek or the twinkle of her silvered eye. Her lost Lenore.

"I thought we were here to *work*?" Ray snaps. "Pick a vid or allow me. Just quit *sighing* already! You wouldn't have had a chance, anyway. She was straighter than Walter."

Root turns the kind of bright scarlet usually reserved for complexions like Ray's.

"How would you know?" she demands. "It's not like you . . ."

Without a word, Ray conjures up the proof: a vid from his own lenses. Night of the intake party, when veteran Voluntolds hazed the fresh batch, then got everyone drunk. A kiss, a sigh, a shift of clothes, a breast, a thigh, more . . .

Root throws both hands out, palms down, fingers spread, and slams them down to hip height. Around them, the vids and holos and tools and all the ephemera of mixed reality slam into the floor, vanishing in virtual dust. They're left standing alone in a drafty outbuilding in Castroville, California, artichoke capital of the world.

"Hey!"

"At least *you'll* remember her. Nightly," Root says, cheeks burning, as she makes an obscene gesture.

"I'm not the only —"

"Fuck *off*, Ray. I'm going to bed."

She's lying. Root crosses from the outbuilding to the cavernous barn, where the arc-light bleeds out under the door. She snaps her hood up just in time.

The light dies, by way of greeting. "You might as well get some sleep," Root says, trying to keep her voice even. "We're not going through with . . ."

"I'm sorry, the hiss of the welder must've given me tinnitus,"

Walter says. His voice *is* even. "I thought I heard you say we're not finishing this."

He gestures to the steel square at his feet, where the lower-left corner still glows orange. Root knows the pattern, even without virtual overlay — there are only a couple pieces left to attach.

"We're not," Root says, biting her lip. "There's nothing to link to the scancode."

"Didn't Ray —"

"*Fuck* Ray!"

Walter is silent. Without a word, he lowers the goggles back down, and sparks the welder. Root barely has time to look away. She screams things into the hiss, but Walter keeps the fire going until Root storms from the barn with tears streaming down her cheeks.

Root wakes with new determination, like an iron ingot in her gut. Hope deserved better. That thought fills her whole headspace; real reasons don't factor into it. She didn't need Ray. She could fill in the last few Modelo details alone over the next few days. Then she and Walter would link it and install it. Yeah, they could still do this.

Curtiss assembles everyone, even Archie Cheong on wash-up detail, straight after breakfast. Thanks to their hard work, — he narrows his eyes at Root — the artichoke harvest's finishing early. Their reward is that they'll be leaving the next morning for Napa and the wage-paid vineyards, instead of getting paid piecework by the 'choke-head.

Root hops off the tractor with a thud and mutters her playlist on. She cranks the volume and goes to work, soil under her nails. She's upset, she forgot gloves. Her mind is scrambling.

At lunch, over Ray's egg-hash, Root finally corners Walter under the tarp.

"We're gonna have to install tonight."

"Thought we weren't doing it," Walter says in the entirely too-calm voice he only uses with Curtiss.

"She deserves better," Root explains. "Better than whatever sticky fantasies are floating around Ray's skull, anyway."

"Funny you mention Ray. I heard something interesting from him this morning."

Root's guts freeze. Her face goes still.

"This isn't about Hope, is it?" Walter says, downing his fork and knife. "This is about *you*."

"What do you —"

"A BQuest account to collect donations from charitably-minded Millennials and iGens." He pops one prematurely-gnarled finger up, then another. And another. "Aggregate data sales to search engines like Informativ or whoever pays most. Trademark rights — Oh yes, I checked local filings. Derivative stats. I'm out of fingers, but I sure as hell ain't out of ideas."

He puts his hand down in a tight, white fist.

"I expected this from Ray. I expected better of *you*." He's trembling, either from too long under hard conditions or from anger.

Root thinks fast. "Ever heard of the boy and the fishes?" she asks. "The tide washed up all the fish on the beach, and the boy starts throwing back all the fish he can pick up. His father asks him, 'there's thousands of fish, what does it matter if you save one or two?' And the boy says —"

"'It matters to *that* one. Yeah." Walter's nostrils flare. "And when you can throw *yourself* back, of course you will."

"A small victory's still a victory."

"'Small' doesn't *have* to mean 'one selfish ass.'"

"Walter, if you wanted a cut . . ."

"Dammit, Root!" Heads of those around them swivel in their direction. Walter lowers his voice. "Root, I had a 3.93 GPA. You graduated *summa cum laude*. You and I aren't here because of personal failings. We're here because the tide washed us up here, you and me and Ray and Bonnie . . . and Hope. The whole fucking 'me first' mentality is what *pulls* that tide."

"I thought you were self-interested American, Exhibit A?"

"You know damn well when I'm being sarcastic." Walter spits. "Even if you toss yourself back, and to Hell with the rest of us, the tide's just gonna wash in again. More kids like Hope are going to *die* under disc harrows, understand? And you're going to call it a victory because that kid *isn't you*."

He sighs. "Root, the woman you *claim* this is all for believed in changing trajectories. How do you think she'd take it that you're not even trying?"

"I *am* changing a trajectory," Root insists. "Mine. That's the American way, right?"

"When you don't like your trajectory, you and your friends build a new rocket, and aim it straight up. *That*'s the American way." With that, Walter snatches up his dirty tin plate, stands, and walks away.

After lunch, Root does something she has never done before. She blinks five times in quick succession, powering down her contacts and the rest, leaving her alone with the soil, and the burning October sun, and artichoke after artichoke after *fucking* artichoke. The cuts that barely healed over lunch split open again under her punishment. They would bleed more before she got on the bus the next morning.

She'd planned a two-man job with Walter to mount the sculpture. It involved four steel I-bars, a StudFinder app, and some spot welding. It involved a lookout, formerly Ray, since the vandalism wasn't as petty as they liked to pretend.

Well, so what if Walter walked. So what if she was alone now. So what if Curtiss had moved up the bus date. Root would make it happen. Somehow. For Hope's sake. And her own.

Without her electronics, Root sees a ghost of Hope Hopkinson working beside her.

· · ·

Root has two bowls of veggie chili for dinner and still finishes before anyone else, even Bonnie. She can't hightail her ass out of the chicken coop fast enough. Root finagles the tractor keys off of the farm manager and unhitches the damn disc harrow. She knows a tractor on the roads around Castroville won't arouse any suspicion. Not even with a brown girl at the wheel.

She sweats, hauling the I-bars to the tractor. She struggles, trundling the welder up to it. But it's the nine-foot-square steel plate with iron ingots welded to it that wrecks her. She grunts, and strains, and slices her fingers open. As soon as it hits loose earth instead of concrete barn floor, Root can't budge the sculpture.

Root's electronics are still off. The questions pop into Root's mind instead of on the search engine's predictive search field. How does she propose to haul the sculpture up the side of a five-story building? How does she propose to attach the sculpture halfway up the side of a five-story building without any welding experience? How does she propose to avoid the police all through this process? How does she look in prison orange? How does she propose to get the sculpture the next *fifty feet* to the tractor?

"Need help?" Ray's voice.

Root's head jerks up, ready to spit fire. Ray preempts her. Ray preempts everybody.

"Wait. Listen to me first," he says. "I'm sorry about last night. I was an ass. It's a cool thing that you're doing, trying to commemorate Hope. There's . . . there isn't a woman on Earth who deserves it more. And I was an ass. I apologize."

He looks away. "I brought help."

Root blinks her contacts back on. The lower left reads 8:04. Then the names pop up. It's hard to read through the tears. There in the darkness are Archie Jeong and Bonnie and Donald and Gary, and even Curtiss. A little ways back, her contacts read "Walter Garcia."

"Thank you." Root gasps. She takes a swig from her battered canteen, and clears her throat. "I can't . . . I'm in fucking *awe* you all came out to help. To remember Hope. Um. Okay. Since we're leaving tomorrow and not Tuesday, we've only got tonight, okay? But I know we can get this thing installed so nobody will ever forget Hope, okay? Okay. Here's how we do . . ."

Root doesn't even notice how much she sounds like Hope right now.

Curtiss stays behind "on Voluntold business," but everyone else climbs onto the tractor or the flatbed that Donald and Gary hitch to the back. Root is about to climb into the driver's seat when a hand claps her shoulder.

"Let's get one thing straight." Walter says. "I'm here for Hope and for all the blood, sweat and tears I put into that goddamn hunk of iron. I'm not here for you. I'm not here for Ray. I'm not here for your fucking payout. I'm here for *her*."

Root's eyes narrow and glow gold in the night.

"Walter . . . wanna drive?" she asks. "I got a few last details to put together."

Walter indeed drives and barks "hold on tight!" Root wraps one hand around the low rail of the flatbed, her eyes opaque and golden. Her other hand dances in the night, weaving, conjuring. She doesn't notice Highway Patrol drive by, when everybody instinctively tenses up. She doesn't notice the bank building lurching up out of the night, the garish blonde hoisting her artichokes with a radiant smile. Her eyes only clear of their opaque golden sheen when Walter pulls to a silent electric stop.

The bank building is the redbrick heart of Castroville, its five stories not even a challenge to onetime intercollegiate free runner Bonnie. Archie spoofs a 911 call to the outskirts of town, a robbery that will draw *both* of Castroville's police cars. Gary and Donald secure the thick chain Bonnie tosses down, and Walter slides his bony ass into a bosun's chair. Between Bonnie, Gary, and Donald, they have everything in place in ten minutes – leaving twenty for Walter to weld the sculpture into place.

Gary spots the studs and knocks out four bricks, exposing the bank's steel bones. Then Walter goes to work, all light and hiss.

In the shadows, Ray and Root conjure a new reality, a new *trajectory*, while sparks fly from the crumbling brick.

"Gotta be open-source," Ray insists.

Root grins. "Raymond Moretti, I didn't know you had it in you."

Archie looks up, ears perked. He has the police band in his soundscape.

"They're coming back," Archie warns to everyone's earband. "Meridian Road's maybe ten minutes away."

"Finito!" Ray says with a shout. Root shushes him. He adds, quieter: "And it's . . . beautiful."

"Ten minutes enough for you guys? Bonnie? Walter?" Root nods to the figures dangling over the side of the building.

"Almost done." Walter's voice is distant, lost in the hiss of sparks. "There! . . . It'll hold."

With ropes, chains, and plenty of hands, they lower Walter in his bosun's chair, then the welder, the ropes, and the chains. Bonnie scuttles down last. She kisses the steel scancode as she passes by, to cheers and laughter. By the time she touches ground, everyone else is already loaded, and she scrambles up onto the flatbed just as Root kicks the tractor's electric engine into gear.

They pass a dented black-and-white electric car at the city limits, and Root watches the sirens light up in the tractor's rearview mirror as it speeds away.

When they make it back to Hall & Sons Produce, Curtiss is standing by the big, beat-up Voluntolds bus.

"Change of plan?" Root asks.

"We might want to get a head start on the Napa grape harvest." Curtiss's face is carefully impassive. "Park the tractor and hop on. Bring your bags."

They pull out of the farm's front gate just as their eyes strike midnight.

When morning dawns, Castroville is all over the virtual world. All eyes are fixed on the side of the bank building where vandals have vandalized a classic mural of Marilyn Monroe in an act of vandalism. Over Marilyn's pretty blonde smile, there is now a steel plate, welded to the building's own support studs that looks like a product scancode. Accepting the scancode transports you to a mixed-reality simulation of an artichoke farm.

In front of you are rows upon rows of artichokes. Go into the first row, and you see still images and short videos, the kind you would see on her social media, of a pretty black girl. Go into the next and you see live video from her friends' contacts as she talks about opening a garage to code classic cars and how much she hates tech support. "Changing trajectory" is like a mantra. She tells off-color jokes and brags about her cooking. Her hands and her eyes are always moving. Go into the last row, and you see only one video: her last few seconds alive, as she slips from the back of an electric tractor toward a hungry disc harrow.

You can pick the artichokes, if you know how. Each artichoke is a dollar. Each artichoke disburses to a random student loan account at Great Lakes. It could be any one of them, just like it could have been any one of them. In the weeks to come, more mystery art appears across the country, seeded and sown by Banksy's bastard children. All of them copy open-source routines from the original, the so-called Castroville Code, disbursing at random among the Voluntolds.

Root's head is thrown back over the bus seat. She's snoring. Vineyards are hard work, even by Voluntold standards. Behind her eyelids, she does not see the dollar debited to her student loan account.

ABOUT R. JEAN MATHIEU

A franco-californien armed with a wok and a word processor, R. Jean Mathieu has hauled sail, served tea, hung beef, sold cell phones, and once even used his own coat as a zip-line sixteen stories above the streets of Hong Kong. He writes every flavor of fiction under a variety of noms de plume. He and his wife, Melissa, keep a good table when not writing side-by-side or chasing trains to the next adventure. You can find Mathieu's award-winning stories in Ecopunk!, Blood on the Floor, RJean-Mathieu.com, and Amazon.com.

THE WELCOMING SKY

CARTER LAPPIN

Sometimes, Orchid still got a little dizzy when she looked up at the sky.

It was just so *big*. Orchid was used to the limits of what she could see being restricted by flat metal ceilings and closed doors. The idea of being able to go outside without some kind of breathing apparatus was horribly foreign and more than a little frightening to a woman who had spent her whole life on a spaceship. Orchid would have felt more silly if she had been the only one to feel like this, but all things told she was doing better than many just by stepping outside and staying there.

So, instead of looking up, Orchid occupied herself by keeping a sharp eye on the various kids scampering across the rolling hills their group had spread out over. She could pick out the youngest in the crowd just by the way they dressed: light, hooded sweaters and the darkest glasses they could get. There had been too many generations that never saw the light of the sun; what had been a useful adaptation onboard the ship now did nothing more than hurt their eyes and prick at their skin.

So far, none of the young ones had gotten themselves into too much trouble. Orchid wasn't the only one keeping watch — every now and then she saw someone herd small clusters of kids back to the main group as they tried to wander off to explore their new home even further. When a group of people shared such tight quarters, communal raising styles were all but inevitable. Orchid had been helping her mom and the other parents with the littler kids since she was hardly older than her younger brother, Road, was now.

Speaking of Road, there he was now, clambering up the grassy hill —and grass, wasn't that a marvel, too? — headed toward where Orchid was sitting with her mother on a blanket spread out over the ground. Orchid noticed with some amusement that his knees were stained green. She hadn't known plants could do that.

Road panted a little as he approached, wound up and unused to the unfiltered atmosphere. "I found a flower." He opened a chubby fist to reveal the delicate greenery, slightly crushed by his clenched hand. "Like you, right?"

Gently, Orchid took the flower into her own hands. It was a small thing with rounded blue petals that were soft to the touch. Orchid had never seen anything like it.

Her namesakes had died out when her ancestors left Earth. Like a lot of people, Orchid had been named after one of the things that had been left behind. She had no idea what any type of flowers would have looked like. Before now, she hadn't seen any outside of the ship's hydroponics bay, and even then there were few to make more room for growing foodstuffs.

Still, she said, "Yeah. Like me."

The colony had only ended their decades-long space journey a few days ago. Generations upon generations of space-travelers, all converging here, now. None of them had ever seen planetfall before. They'd perfected the art of living in a traveling colony-ship, now all they had to do was figure out how to live without it. All they'd had to go on were nostalgia-tinted stories passed down from generation to generation, faded with time and distance.

But they'd made it. An inhabitable planet, thousands of miles away from where they'd set out from. Sometimes, Orchid still couldn't believe it happened in her lifetime. It had always seemed like such a distant dream, a fairy tale she'd read to her brother when the designated night-cycles were long and he couldn't sleep.

The ship had set down nearby, the vessel that had been so many people's home now being slowly dismantled as permanent structures were created from its bones. If she craned her head, Orchid could just about see the top of it, shining silver in the light.

Most of the colony had stayed in orbit for a week while the first team went down to confirm the planet's habitability in person, rather than the long-distance probe images they'd been going off of. All things told, the new home planet wasn't that much different from the one they'd left, albeit minus a couple hundreds of thousands of years of human interference. It was like the Earth had been once before. Or so Orchid had been told. Twelve generations had been born and died since there was last someone who knew what Earth had been like in person.

Likewise, things her ancestors would have once taken as a given were new and wondrous to their descendants. Things like open skies and plants growing without limitations and the unfiltered light of the sun. And weather. That was a big one. It was why everyone was here right now, actually.

They were so deep into space. And yet this planet was so much like home. What home would have been like had Orchid been born on Earth instead of a spaceship amongst the shining stars. One day, Orchid's descendants would look back at this uncertain time and think of it as distant history, too.

Until then, there was the rain.

The settlement planet, while like Earth in most ways, had a few quirks all to itself. Its rotation around the sun was a little slower, its oceans a little deeper. And the rain fell once every three days, always at the same time.

The scientists called it a meteorological marvel. Orchid's mother called it a blessing. Orchid thought they both might be right. It didn't rain on spaceships. She wondered what it was like. Nobody else knew, either.

Today, for the first time in a long, long time, humankind would experience the rain.

They had all gathered for it, young and old, and half-blinded by an unfiltered sun and dizzied by a sky that seemed to stretch out forever. Most, like Orchid and her mom, had brought a blanket of some kind, uncertain about sitting on the new grass. Several had brought along jars as well, poised with their lids off to catch the water when it started to fall. There wasn't any real reason for it, just sentiment, wanting to keep a little piece of wonder stashed away. Every so often a beam of sunlight would catch a glass mason jar at just the right angle and send washes of warm light over the crowd.

Road had wandered away again, satisfied with Orchid's response — or maybe just bored. Orchid couldn't blame him. There was so much to see. Orchid couldn't imagine that her little colony would ever manage to see anything all. Maybe one day. Perhaps even in Road's lifetime. Orchid liked the thought of that.

This time, when Orchid cast an uncertain gaze upwards, the sky had started to take on a gray tint. Clouds had crept in while she wasn't looking. The shapes were wonderful, but Orchid had to look away again before the true vastness of the sky could sink in.

"Not long now," her mother murmured from her place on the blanket. When Orchid looked over, her mother's face was unreadable.

"What do you think the rain will feel like?" Orchid asked to break the strange mood.

Her mother upturned her hand, like she was imagining catching falling rain on it. "Cold, perhaps," she said. "I'd never thought to imagine. I didn't think I would ever see it."

Orchid thought she knew what her mother meant. She glanced up at the sky again, and it was gray. Nearly the same color as the metal ceiling in her room on the ship had been. Huge and unknowable and so much. She closed her eyes.

A tap at her forehead. Orchid opened her eyes. All around

her, excited cries were beginning to rise up from the crowd. The rain had started.

The sky seemed to open up. Water fell in fat, heavy drops, soaking into Orchid's clothes and hair. She jumped as a droplet found its way down the back of her neck, then laughed at herself. The rain was indeed cold, but not uncomfortably so. It was soothing, like a hand on her forehead in the midst of a fever.

It was pouring. The sound of the rain hitting the ground was almost musical. Orchid laughed again, filled with joy. It was raining. For the first time Orchid knew rain, and she loved it.

Road had frozen where he stood and was looking up at the sky in awe, the water beading on the lenses of his dark glasses. For once, he was still.

All around them, people were moving. Some had gotten up from their blankets, holding their arms out and their heads tilted upwards as though to make sure the rain got to them as quickly as possible. A nearby couple had started to dance, a stumbling sort of two-step that involved the two of them clinging to each other as the rain fell around them. Rain clattered against jars as they were slowly filled.

Someone, somewhere, was singing. It was too indistinct for Orchid to make out any real words, but the tone was clear anyways. Happiness. Wonder. For the first time in so long, humanity knew the rain, and they loved it.

Generation after generation had traveled so far, sacrificed so much. Orchid thought that it all must have been worth it, to have culminated in something as beautiful as this.

Rain on a new planet. A new place to call home. The air was full of joy, and Orchid looked up.

The sky was gray and full of clouds. Orchid found that she wasn't as frightened of it anymore. She was home, and it was raining. The world seemed suddenly full of possibility.

ABOUT CARTER LAPPIN

Carter Lappin is a Californian author. Her works of fiction have appeared in publications such as Apparition Lit, Air and Nothingness Press, Dreadstone Press, Manawaker Studio, and World-Weaver Press. You can find her on Twitter at @CarterLappin.

THE THIRD PLACE

EMMA SLOLEY

We live in the hotel now. The one on 38th with the busted angel fountain. It was once a place for business people to stay when they were in the city. When we first found it years ago, there were couches set up as workstations and an area where people could make coffee and tea from little sachets. We repurposed the couches and drank the last of the coffee, pretending to be executives barking into phones because that world had vanished so recently it was funny rather than poignant to think about it.

The lobby looks different today. Tents pitched all over the fake marble floors. Play areas heaped with cushions and toys. The walls are covered with questionable art hung at eccentric angles. What was once the check-in desk is now a library crammed with books people have found around the city. Some of the books are warped and buckled from being in the rain.

I waged a campaign in the early days to call our new home The Last Resort, but it never caught on. I think they all objected to the pun. Not the renaming, because we rename things all the time. Like Solace — that's what we call the city even though it used to go by another name. I can't remember what the original name was. Sometimes it's better not to remember, to tuck the knowledge away in some dark corner, like a librarian filing something that will never be needed again but can't be thrown away for complicated and arcane reasons. The old names conjure thoughts that aren't always happy. The new name emerges squeaky clean from history. Tabula rasa.

At first, we kept on living purely out of spite. But after a while it began to seem like a good idea in its own right. With so much room to spread out, you'd think we would have staked individual claims on our favored corners of the abandoned city. Instead, we peons returned like sleepwalkers to the forced intimacies of communal living.

All over the city there are little communities like ours, mostly in hotels. There's a comfort in it. This way, we're all learning together. We older citizens tack our clumsy ideas of how the world once worked onto this new framework, but the kids have tapped into fonts of innate knowledge so old they feel new again. They have a special genius for knowing the phases of the moon and the tides. Soon they'll be able to steer their boats by the stars, should they find a boat and wish to steer it somewhere.

Today is the last Tuesday of the month, the day the guards leave their skyscraper to distribute medicine. I wake before the alarm goes off, staring for a long time at the cracked plaster ceiling because I'm nervous and excited. At forty-one years old I'm considered an elder. The younger members of our pack have decided I'm entitled to the luxury of a hotel room all to myself, and despite my explaining the importance of dissolving the hierarchical structures of the past, they insist. I can't say I hate it: the wide bed and the window that looks out over a multi-story parking lot, its concrete curves furred with moss. I close my eyes tight and as sometimes happens, an image appears of a murmuration of starlings blackening the sky. When I open my eyes again the scene in front of me wavers like looking through a car wash, as if it's *this* world that isn't real.

We all gather in the lobby to travel to the drop-off site. It's more efficient to go as a pack so everyone can sift through and find the specific medicines they need. There is a list. Someone needs a new asthma inhaler. A few people need heart meds. We always need sterile bandages, sutures, antiseptic, and painkillers for all the cuts or scrapes that come from living and foraging inside a crumbling metropolis. It used to be easier to find this stuff back when the city first emptied out and you could just wander into a pharmacy and take what you needed from the shelves, but the shelves are mostly empty now.

We exit the lobby into the mild sunshine. It won't reach one hundred degrees until later in the afternoon, and I find myself enjoying the feeling of sun on my skin and the festival atmosphere attending our outing. As we walk, a few of us return to the question of why this medicine drop is happening. They introduced it six months ago, but they didn't tell us why. Ulises thinks it's because the aristos don't want to look down and see bodies fouling up their view. Or they worry that sickness on the ground could invade their world. Or there's actually a slow-working poison or a sterilizing agent and they're trying to kill us off. Jules, whose optimism could power the whole city, claims it's because the aristos want us to thrive, and they know we can't make the medicine ourselves.

"Yet," trills Nadina, our resident chemist/mycologist, who's working on developing medicines from molds, fungi, and mycelium in the makeshift research lab we stocked with equipment taken from the abandoned university.

I'm not sure what to think. My primary mission today is to grab some antibiotics because one of the kids has an infected tooth, but my secret, secondary mission is to catch a glimpse of my younger brother, Ant, who lives in a skyscraper called AZ 128. (AZ stands for Autonomous Zone, but we peons don't call it that.) When the aristos swapped the earth for the clouds, they recruited a select number of us to fill the lowlier roles, like security guards and cleaners. Ant clamored for the chance. I tried to talk him out of it. I begged and pleaded, but he wouldn't be swayed. He'd always been like that, stubborn and proud.

Most of us were scared of the new world they are making up in the skyscrapers. We preferred scrabbling around on what was left of this earth. But Ant was on fire with the idea of living above the inversion layer — a thick layer of smog that divides the cities above and below. He wouldn't rest until he was imprisoned inside a starched uniform and disappearing through those tinted doors. The elevator spirited him to the hundredth floor of the building, or the two hundredth, I don't even know how many floors there are in most of the skyscrapers. They glitter so brightly in the sun it hurts my eyes as their monstrous shadows darken the streets below.

After someone claims the sky, it kind of changes how you see yourself in relation to the world. The aristos didn't bother issuing many rules to those left behind, but we understood. Don't try to rise any higher than the ground. Don't even joke about collecting some ropes and crampons and climbing the side of a building until you get to the real world up there. Don't even think about it. You'd be vaporized before you even got your first foothold. What would you do once you got there anyway? There are pigeon spikes on all the windows and balconies, except they're not for pigeons. There are none of those left.

I talk about birds like I remember them, but the truth is I don't. The big die-off happened when I was younger than any of these kids. Rumor has it there are still some species out in the campo. They have everything out there, apparently, but like the skyscrapers, it's off limits to us peons. My whole life, the narrative was all about how bad the cities were: cesspools of vice and filth, crime-ridden hellholes, godless places. The campo, by contrast, took on an aura of virtue. People of means shunned the urban centers, flooding into the countryside and building gates and walls to keep out any peons who might get it in their filthy heads to do the same.

Solace grew more chaotic and noisy for a while, but then it grew quieter and quieter, even after the aristos moved back in. They moved so far up they were basically on another plane of existence altogether. And within that new quiet I could hear myself think. Which is a boon, apart from when the quiet reminds me that I haven't heard a bird in a long time.

As we pass through the shadow of a skyscraper, I bend to scoop up the train of the wedding veil Libby is wearing before it trails in a puddle. The delicate embroidered lace is so worn it's translucent in places. Droplets cling to its fibers like a spider's web. It's so beautiful that a feeling of sadness catches in my throat. I often have these moments now. Attacks of sentiment, I suppose. They tend to arrive on the heels of situations like this, witnessing the pack bedecked in all their finery, as colorful and flamboyant as tropical birds in their huge crumpled hats, threadbare ballgowns, vibrant silk turbans, and T-shirts emblazoned with the logos of dead companies. Beaded necklaces, combat pants beneath tutus, anything goes. The clothes come from dusty closets and the deserted halls of department stores. The aristos left everything behind they didn't want, so it's not even stealing. Just repurposing.

"This reminds me of Mardi Gras," I say to Yasha, who has been keeping step beside me in companionable silence.

"What's that?" He pushes a pair of angel wings back off his shoulders. They look to be constructed from an old bed sheet stretched across two racket heads and attached to a harness he wears snug across his chest. The rackets set off a small clangor in my brain. Was there really a game called squash or am I hallucinating that? He looks at me expectantly, as if he really wants to hear.

I hesitate, wondering if I even know anymore. "Well. I think it was a kind of street festival celebrating . . . something. I read about it in a book."

Yasha nods solemnly in spite of my unsatisfying answer. He's such a polite kid. He respects the need we elders have to share our decomposing memories of the time before. He darts off to take a photograph of something he's spotted in a busted old gas station. Yasha's superpower is finding beauty in the things the rest of us overlook. Everyday artifacts: a snarl of tangled electrical wires like a Medusa head, a sagging awning cracked and bleached by the sun, ragged strips snapping like fingers in the wind, a blue plastic bucket wedged in a drain swollen with debris. He sets out each day to document the world. He is so pure of heart I ache with worry for him.

There are still so many cars in the street. We have to thread our way through them, a little trail of insects to anyone watching from on high. My heart skitters as we approach the skyscraper in which Ant lives. It's one of the newest and fanciest, with everything from vast air farms to burlesque halls, if you believe the stories. Enclosed bridges run between it and the other skyscrapers. I squint up at its sheer black and silver sides. The bulk of the upper stories are obscured by the inversion layer. It looks benign, almost approachable, when you can only see a fragment of it. Incredible to think how many people live up there now, sealed off from the ruined world below. Impossible to imagine their days.

I've timed it perfectly because at the very moment I stop, Ant emerges from the lobby of AZ 128. He walks in loose sync with half a dozen other guards, two of whom push the carts full of medicine. It's only a few blocks to the gutted supermarket where they drop the meds. We walk after them, keeping a respectable distance. The guards always seem jumpy and scared around us, as if we pose some kind of threat.

I keep my eyes fixed on Ant's straight back. He is bristling with weaponry, things I've never even seen before. It makes me shiver. The way we're always dreaming up new ways of harming one another. Not we, though. Not us; not anymore. I can tell he's spotted me because he keeps sending tiny staccato glances over his left shoulder, and he's walking carefully and nervously as though he's balancing a fragile item on the crown of his head. I speed up to get alongside him. He nonchalantly moves closer, keeping his eyes trained on the guard in front of him. "Do you need anything?"

He always asks this, and I never quite know how to answer. *I need to know they're not mistreating you. I need you not to be as lonely as your eyes suggest you are. I need you to come back.* But I don't say any of this. I can't square this tough soldier with the soft kid who used to keep a tattered encyclopedia of birds beneath his pillow, pouring over the faded pages in case he ever saw a bird and needed to identify it on the spot. I tell him we're fine, and that's largely true. There's nothing he could procure for us up there that wouldn't put his safety in jeopardy.

"Are you —" I begin, but someone shoves me from behind and I stumble. Another one of the guards.

"Move it," he says. Not even meanly, very mild and unconcerned, like I'm a piece of debris in his path. I veer away, trying to make eye contact with Ant one last time but he's looking straight ahead like he's scared to be associated with me, which is probably close to the truth, so I don't say anything more, just slink away.

We return to the hotel, arms loaded with bounty. Everyone leaves the meds lined up on the concierge desk for me to file, then they disperse to begin their various tasks. Xin sets up her tattoo station in the small room off the lobby she claimed years ago for the purpose. She already has people waiting because her ink work is legendary. There are people in our pack whose entire bodies are artworks-in-progress, and while it's not for me, I admire the commitment to putting so much literal skin in the game. A large group of gardeners led by Arturo departs to work on the canchés, the ancient Mayan raised garden beds where we grow most of our food. Arturo had the idea to build them as a way to avoid the poisoned, nutrient-depleted soils, and they've flourished under the gardeners' care.

"Hey, captain," says Gray, one of our kitcheners, glancing at the tattered concierge sign and sliding a bag of meds across. "Always behind that desk."

I smile, embarrassed, and stoop to slot the meds in the pigeonhole marked with Gray's name. I set up this filing system to keep track of everyone's things. "It reminds me of having an office job," I say. "Can you believe people used to get paid to stand behind here all day?" I mean the question to sound incredulous, but it comes out wistful instead.

"You should join us in the kitchen," Gray says. "We can always use another set of hands, and we have a lot of fun."

I nod as if giving it thought because I don't want to offend him by saying I much prefer my position here. But it's true you can be anything now — a cook, an anthropologist, a photographer, a tree climber, a seamstress, a musician, a stargazer, a puddle-jumper. Or a concierge in a world where hotels no longer have any reason to exist.

"I don't like the idea of working," Gray says. I start, because I hadn't even realized he was still there. He lays his forearm along the counter as if he's settling in for the day. "Sounds boring, if you ask me."

I laugh. "But you *do* work. It's just work you enjoy and choose to do, so it doesn't feel like work."

"I guess when you put it that way," he says with a grin, adjusting his bowler hat and turning to leave.

I suddenly don't want to be left alone with my thoughts, and I blurt out, "That actually reminds me . . . there used to be this thing called a third place. Somewhere that's not work or home but another space, where people go to be alone or find community or just hang out. Just, I don't know, a place to contemplate the world without all the other distractions."

Gray looks at me quizzically for a little bit, no doubt wondering where I get these notions. Then he shrugs, takes his hat off and swirls it expertly on his pointer finger. "The whole world is a third place now, Cap."

Beyond the calm order of my concierge desk, chaos pulses like floodwater. The children have taken over. They draw and paint on every surface they can find. They make sculptures out of discarded things. They chatter like sparrows, growl like predators. I smile at the thoughtless pleasure they take in being their physical selves, sleek and fast and antic like sea otter cubs rolling through the water. I try to avoid scolding them, even when they're doing something dangerous or annoying. Only if there's true risk of mortal harm will I step in. If one of them is hurt or sad or overwhelmed I offer condolences of whatever kind best suits them — a hug, a pep talk, something sweet, a quiet corner on their own. Once there were people who believed in raising children via something called tough love. A kind of test to see if the child was worthy. But that's all gone now. In this hotel you don't have to prove you deserve love.

After I've finished behind the concierge desk, I wander out to see about some other tasks I've been meaning to do. But a malaise comes over me, a sense of hopelessness born out of my encounter with Ant. I wander barefoot to the courtyard, the veins of cracked concrete rough under my feet. I drop an inflatable mattress in the pool and flop facedown onto it, arms outstretched. I don't care that my fingers trail in the slimy, scum-lined surface of the water. I don't care that a noxious smell wafts out of the nearby water tank, like something fell in it and drowned. I don't care that my skin will burn in minutes beneath the scorching sun. May as well just float here and let the world go on without me.

Sometime during this wallowing session, Yasha returns and sits silently by the pool. He has changed outfits since this morning and is now wearing a long pale-yellow kaftan-like garment that swamps his narrow frame.

"You remind me of one of those cult leaders," I drawl, shading my eyes from the dazzle of the sun. "Ready to lead your people into the desert."

He looks up, smiling. "Want to see something cool?"

Belly-down, I paddle my mattress lazily to the edge of the pool and stretch my hand out to take the device at which Yasha is lovingly staring. He hands it to me. I look at what is on the screen: a large bird, perhaps as tall as a toddler, with a bald head and a long yellow curved beak. Its white feathers are tinged with pink at the end, as though the creature just brushed past fresh paint or emerged from a minor fight. I scroll to see if there are more photos, and there are. I can feel Yasha's intense gaze on the side of my face.

"How did you do this?"

"Do what?"

"Make it look so real."

"It is real."

"But there's nothing like that. Never was." I don't know why I say this. Or why my voice is sharp with anger. He looks calmly at me, then gives his shoulders a little shimmy and turns away. I've seen him do this before. It's how he shakes off negativity. I clamber out of the pool, almost slipping as I lurch after him. "Wait!" Yasha turns obediently. I flick my wrists to remove the last droplets of fetid water. "You saw this with your real eyes?"

He laughs and points to his eyes. "Correct."

"Listen, can I come back there with you next time you go? I want to see it for myself."

"Of course. We should bring everyone."

"You're right, sorry." I hate that my first thought was to hoard, like the aristos do. "Yes, everyone. Tomorrow?"

He nods and wanders off unhurried, his serene face raised, ready to receive whatever the day's next miracle might be.

My legs carry me with dream-like ease back inside, my mind still stuck on the bird. I can't believe it. I don't even know its name. I just know it's the most magnificent and preposterous thing I've ever seen, and I have spent a lifetime witnessing preposterous things. But by the time I get back to the lobby, I'm breathless with the prospect of seeing it in the flesh.

"Eight minutes!"

As the words ring out, everyone snaps into action. Gray has a gift when it comes to sensing the arrival of the daily monsoon, and he's never wrong. That means we have about eight minutes to get under cover anything we don't want drowned or blown away. The canchés are the most important, and we all run outside to help the gardeners move our mobile milpa under cover. Arturo and his team put wheels on the raised planters so they're easy to move in and out of the parking lot next to the hotel. The wind is already so fierce it could snatch the eyelashes right off your face.

"You know what?" I yell cheerfully to Han, who's pushing a canché next to me.

"Let me guess. This reminds you of something from the old times?" He screws up his face in a grin to show he's just teasing. They know me too well. By the time everything is under cover, the monsoon has begun and I've already forgotten the story I was going to tell. The rain comes down in opaque sheets that can drench you to the skin in five seconds flat. We stand in groups chatting, a few people smoking some experimental weed they've cultivated.

Never one to give up in the face of friendly indifference, I sidle up to a nearby kid. "This reminds me of a car wash," I say as we watch the torrential rain pelt down. "That's where people used to go to have machines wash their cars for them."

I may as well be talking to myself. It's not so bad. You get used to absences quicker than you think you will. You get used to everything quicker than you think you will.

The monsoon stops abruptly. Those few minutes after it stops are one of the best times of the day. What at first feels like silence soon resolves into a quiet symphony of dripping and the far-off rushing of water in the culverts. The air is fresh and pleasantly cool for a little while until the sun begins to bake everything again and the atmosphere recommences shimmering. Into this dripping world arrives a sense of newness, as after a baptism.

Evening is another good time, after we've washed up and are sitting on the roof of the hotel watching the wild spectacle that is the sunset. All around, the skyscrapers glitter with light.

"I've heard they have tigers in the penthouse up there," says Xin dreamily, chin pointed at the sky. "A rhino in the ballroom. Can you imagine?" The people within earshot nod or laugh or fall contemplative, depending on their tolerance for fantasy.

. . .

For the second night in a row, I can't sleep. I want to see the bird, but I'm afraid too. Because what if it's not real, or what if it has one of those avian flus and we have to put it to sleep?

In the morning, Yasha leads us to the place, a site four avenues away and many city blocks north. As we walk, I keep a wary eye on the sky for any harbingers of a monsoon. It's harder to take shelter quickly when you don't know an area well. But the sky stays clear.

Yasha pulls aside a gap in a hurricane fence so we can all step through into a huge vacant lot scattered with ancient garbage. At the center is a pond fouled by algae and debris. He puts his finger to his lips and begins to walk quietly to the edge, then steps aside so we can all see. I clamp my hand to my mouth, fearing the sound I might make could scare it away.

Gleaming against the muck, the bird's feathers are as bright as jewels. It picks its way on delicate pink legs through the swamp like a socialite wending through a party, foraging happily away. Taking no notice of us.

On the walk home, as our own flock chatters excitedly about the birds, Yasha catches up to me and says quietly, "There are more, you know."

I turn and stare at him, my fingers digging into his wrist. "What? Where?"

He rubs his lips together, then smiles bashfully, as if hesitant to boast. "Everywhere. I mean, not *everywhere*, but all over, in little pockets of the city where there's enough food and water."

"But what about the toxins? The poison?"

He shrugs. "I don't know. Maybe the levels have subsided. They must know."

I blink, trying to process it.

"I know," Yasha says, linking his arm through mine. "It's a lot. I didn't want to believe it at first."

"We have to find them all," I say, in a kind of fever now.

"Yes," Yasha says, and he looks the happiest I've ever seen him. "It's not only the painted storks. I've looked them all up. There are warblers and bar-tailed godwits. A whole flock of ducks in the south. Ibis. Pied avocets." He savors these strange exotic words like they're edible delicacies.

Every day after that, we set off as soon as the monsoon has passed to look at the birds. In some places they whiten the sky, great flocks of them like hope taking flight. Someone returns from a solo foray with tales of a downy pileated woodpecker tapping insistently at an old power line. We swap our sightings around the fire pit and by candlelight on the rooftop. Libby records them all, and the ones we can't identify we invent new names for.

The last Tuesday of the month rolls around. On our medicine run, I see my brother again. As has become our custom, I find a way to subtly sidle close to him. This time when he asks if there's anything I need, I silently show him the screen in my palm. He glances at it and his dark eyes widen. The muscles in his neck jump.

"How did you do this?" The very thing I had asked Yasha the first time.

"It's real," I say quickly because we don't have much time.

A light comes into his face then, a memory being dredged up of a thing he once valued. A yearning, maybe. "Where on —" He begins, but another soldier barks some instruction to him and he moves off. I don't know if I've quite gotten through to him. I hope it's enough.

After we return to the hotel and our tasks are completed, we break into smaller packs to go birdwatching. Yasha and I end up sitting together on a miraculously unrusted oil barrel near an industrial site we both like. There is a large pond streaked with iridescent rainbows and more and more birds descend upon it each day. A few of the children play nearby. Behind them, a row of skyscrapers looms against a curdled sky. We appreciate the birds in silence for a while, and then Yasha turns to me.

"They left us to die but instead we ended up being the ones who lived."

He has a poet's soul so it's not unusual for him to say things like this, but I feel as though I've stopped listening lately. I squeeze his hand to let him know I'm listening now, and he squeezes mine back.

One of the kids runs over, her grubby once-white dress hiked up around her thighs. It is Faydra, an eight-year-old whose sartorial instincts are impressive even by our pack's standards. Her hair is fixed in the most elaborate style I've ever seen, all whorls and perfect rows of braids threaded through with pearls.

"Would you tie my ribbon," she asks me imperiously, presenting her skinny neck, where a velvety ribbon has come partly loose and is flapping in the breeze.

I pull her closer and carefully tie the ribbon back in a neat bow.

"Look!" She points out toward the swampy wasteland. "An egret!" The kids have all become ornithologists overnight.

"So it is," I say. "You know what this reminds me of?"

Faydra twists her beribboned neck to look up at me. "What?"

I open my mouth to respond but my throat is dry and the words don't come. I pull her tight against me and ruffle up her hair until she squeals at me that she's spent all morning getting it just perfect and I'm so disrespectful. She runs off pouting but not really upset, just trying on a mood like you do as a kid. An abundance of wild joy unspools inside me for the first time in as long as I can remember. Because you know what?

It doesn't remind me of anything.

ABOUT EMMA SLOLEY

Emma Sloley's fiction and creative non-fiction has appeared in Catapult, Literary Hub, Yemassee journal, Joyland, The Common, Structo, and the Masters Review Anthology, among many others. Emma is also a MacDowell fellow and a Bread Loaf scholar, and her debut novel, DISASTER'S CHILDREN, was published by Little A books in 2019. Born in Australia, she now divides her time between the US and the city of Mérida, Mexico. You can find Emma on Twitter @Emma_Sloley and www.emmasloley.com

TEA AND TREASURES

RAVEN J. DEMERS

Cora entered her parents' home for the first time in almost forty years. Little had changed: The same brown recliner, now threadbare, that her father sat in every evening reading the paper. The same porcelain knickknacks on the open shelves between the living room and kitchen now sported a thin layer of dust. Even the smell kindled a mixture of emotions. Tears welled in the corners of her eyes, but she blinked them back.

Before she could assess what to keep and what to discard, she walked through the house, room by room. Some things had changed. When had her parents started sleeping in separate rooms? When had her bedroom been turned into a crafting room?

Cora stood still in the doorway, trying to see the room as it was in her teens. Behind the sewing machine and serger, behind the neatly folded stacks of fabric and narrow shelves full of color-coordinated cases of threads, bobbins, and notions, Cora caught small glimpses of her faded wallpaper.

She crossed the room to her old closet and opened the door. On the back of it was the poem she'd written for Jackie Guerra in her junior year still burned deep into the wood where her mother tried and failed to paint over it. Those woodshop classes came in handy for more than just getting close to Jackie.

"Hey, mom," a voice said, startling Cora from her wistful nostalgia.

Cora pressed a hand to her chest and turned enough to see M — no, that's not their name anymore, she reminded herself. "You startled me, honey."

"Sorry about that. Where did you want me to start?" Their hair fell thick and black in front of their face.

"I was going to say the attic, but I'm worried you won't be able to see in front of you," Cora said with a laugh.

"Pfft. I'll be fine, Mom," Florian said and blew a strand of hair away from the front of their mouth, giving her a winning smile.

Cora returned to the living room, taping up boxes. She wished Navi were there with her. Of all the times her mother had to die, it had be seven months *after* the divorce finalized.

Florian appeared in the room. "There isn't much of use in the attic. I can't believe the broken garbage they left up there, but I found this box with what I'm guessing was your stuff."

When they set the box down, a thick cloud of dust rose causing them both to sneeze. Cora eased herself onto her knees and tore the tape off the box, opening a host of memories. Every photo her parents ever took of her: every trophy, every drawing that once graced the refrigerator door had been crammed into cardboard and sealed up so they could forget about her. "They must have given away my clothes . . . and tossed my journals," Cora muttered as she took each scrap of her childhood from the box. The tears fell freely now, and Florian placed a comforting hand on her shoulder.

"I'll get us something to drink, Mom."

Cora reached to the bottom and retrieved her old jewelry box. She sat back, causing her hips to pop in protest. She lifted the lid and there, exactly where she left it, was her most treasured possession. She thought it had been lost.

She threaded her fingers beneath the silver chain with care and lifted the necklace until the pendant hung in the air. A translucent white stone hoop embedded with filaments of green moss caught the sunlight pouring through the windows and seemed to glow of its own accord.

Florian returned with a glass of water and a can of lemonade iced tea. "Pick your poison. They're both tepid. Ooh, what's that?"

Cora's face beamed up at her only child. "A gift from a dear friend I met in the woods long ago." Cora absentmindedly accepted the water and added, "It's magic."

"Do you think she'll notice?" Florian asked. They concentrated on their reflection while they dabbed foundation on their face, sucking in pain through their teeth.

Glory perched on the counter to face them. "She's your mom."

"Right." Florian sighed. "Forget it. Maybe I'll just try a new hairstyle," they said, throwing a hunk of hair in front of the oblong bruise across their eye, forehead, and cheek. "At least the shirt covers the rest."

"I can call in sick. Come with you. Lifting boxes with those bruises —"

"No," Florian said, kissing Glory's cheek. "She's my mom, and this is my fault."

"The fuck it is, Flor. Those douche nozzles started it."

Florian took Glory's hand. "And I finished it." They smirked beneath the curtain of hair.

"What about Navi?" Glory asked with a hopeful look. "Surely she'd show up to support you."

Florian stepped out of the bathroom and grabbed their phone. "Maa doesn't think Mom would want her there."

"She ought to be there for you; she's your mother, too."

"I know, Glory, but she's not even in the country right now.

She's on another research trip in some Brazilian forest." Florian swallowed down the pain of her absence. "Babe, we'll be okay."

Glory took off her shamrock ring and placed it on Florian's ring finger. "For luck." She kissed Florian firmly before sending them out to meet their mom.

It took most of the day, three blocks of sticky notes, and a roll of tape to go through all the objects held within her childhood home. Cora felt overwhelmed. She left to grab takeout from the Korean restaurant six blocks away, and as she walked back to the house, a withered man peered out at her from his front door.

He waved a cane in her direction. "Aren't you Cora Jones?"

Her back stiffened with surprise to see him still alive after so long, but she kept her leisurely pace toward the house. "It's Cora Laghari now, Mr. Whitecastle."

"You have a lot of nerve returning. Broke your father's heart," he said as she passed his porch.

She paused, heat rising in her chest, and faced him. "Funny, I heard his heart kept ticking just fine another thirty-eight years after he tossed me out on the street."

His jaw worked over some musty retort, but she continued on her way, throwing a, "Good evening, Mr. Whitecastle," over her shoulder and lightly touched the hoop stone hanging from her neck.

Cora laid out the food back at the house, not saying a word of the neighbor's comments to Florian. They shared a meal, talked of what was to be done with the objects in the house, and Glory arrived to offer Florian a ride home.

"Are you staying?" Florian asked.

"There are a few more things I need to look over before I leave."

Florian hesitated. "Won't you need help loading the car?"

"No, honey. You head home with Glory and get some rest.

Thank you for your help today; I don't think I could have gone through all of this alone." She touched her child's arm and reached to stroke their hair, but Florian flinched back. "What's wrong?"

"Nothing," Florian lied, but Glory muttered something. "I'll be fine. Just a disagreement about my existence."

Cora frowned with concern. "What do you mean, a disagreement? What are you hiding?"

"I need to go, Mom. I'll call you tomorrow, okay? Don't stay here too long; it's too toxic," Florian said, backing toward Glory's car with their hands firmly in their pockets.

Cora stood on the porch, her arms empty, her nose full of her child's scent fading in the evening breeze. Her frown didn't ease even as she waved goodbye to the car pulling away.

Florian sank down in their seat and held out their palm to the window, not daring to meet their mother's eyes.

Cora sighed and touched the stone again, remembering why she lingered in the house of her horrific childhood. In every step, she recalled the quiet tension, the flurries of anger when breaking from control, the tears. She also remembered her respite.

Cora stood on the concrete that comprised the narrow back porch, staring at the dark line of trees at the end of the yard. Weeds had cropped up between the pansies in her mother's single flower bed. The asparagus had claimed a corner of the house, obscuring her father's bedroom window. Morning glory and sweet pea vines fought for control of the chain link fence.

One of the benefits of growing up on the edge of town was having a forest for a backyard and a stream along which she had chased frogs, dragonflies, and dreams.

She took a single step onto dewy grass, refreshing on her bare feet. Without a candle or flashlight, Cora walked slowly through the uncut grass, her hand wrapped around the stone. At the first poplar, she paused and held up the pendant, looking through the large hole at its center. The woods danced with specks of light where fireflies had long since been absent, and a warmer breeze blew between the trees, beckoning her in.

"I've lost my mind," she said with a chuckle and a smile.

"Have you?" asked a quiet voice from a branch above her. A shadowy figure coiled down the trunk of the tree and landed before her. "How lovely. Here I thought you had merely forgotten me."

Cora's breath caught as she faced the person she had thought was her imaginary friend — a friend who lingered long after everyone else had outgrown theirs. Her therapist had called them a coping mechanism.

"Treyva," Cora breathed. She peered at them through the stone and saw their skin shining lavender and their eyes glowing yellow.

Their warm, slender fingers touched the hand that held the stone. "At least you still have my gift."

"I lost it for a time," Cora guiltily admitted. Until that morning, when Florian brought down the box from the attic, she had forgotten it entirely. "You haven't aged a day." She held her tongue about how short Treyva seemed after over forty years.

"You have grown into a giant . . . and you had the poor manners to grow old," Treyva said, playfully wrinkling their nose.

Cora snorted a laugh.

Treyva took her hand, and she no longer required the stone to see the lights of the forest. "Tell me," they started, "did you convince Jackie Guerra to run away with you?"

"Ah, no. Her face turned gray when I confessed my feelings," Cora recounted.

Treyva considered. "What a shame. You are behind on your lessons. You have much to catch up on and we have little time left to us." They led her down the path toward the stream and over into their realm, talking most of the night.

In the fading blue of pre-dawn, Cora left her parents' house for the movers and the realtor to handle, carrying out only a book of photos and the pendant hanging around her neck, feeling lighter than she'd had in almost fifty years.

Florian ended the call and rubbed the bridge of their nose.

"Who was that?" Glory set down the box she'd been carrying toward the stockroom.

Florian spun in the chair. "The realtor. The grands' house sold, but mom can't be reached. Again."

Glory sighed. "You have to go down there again? The grand opening is in three days!"

"I know, babe. I'll be back in an hour, maybe two if they forget how to sign their names," Florian said, snatching up the car keys and heading for the front door. "If the delivery from Hastings comes in while I'm away, send me a text."

Glory agreed and continued to the backroom to stock supplies.

Florian's heavy steps on the pavement beat in time to their frustrated huffs. Cora had always been a tad eccentric, but over the past several months, she started taking frequent trips to other countries using up the money she inherited from their retirement fund, and probate hadn't even closed!

They adjusted the mirrors to de-Glorify the car to suit their stature better and tapped Cora's name on the phone screen. Voicemail. *Again.* "You couldn't even wait until all the papers were signed, mom? I have responsibilities! You can't just keep foisting yours onto me." They pulled out into traffic. "I don't know if this is some mid-life crisis thing or grief or what, but . . ." Florian sighed once more. "I'd hoped you'd at least be here for the opening."

With nothing more to say and no one to hear their words, Florian cranked the radio's volume until they felt the beat in their bones and hit the accelerator.

No one answered the door at the house, and Florian's cheeks

grew hot upon realizing they didn't need to wait to enter. Until the papers were signed, the house still technically belonged to their mom. At first, it seemed the house was entirely empty, but two cars sat on the street outside. Inside, a folding table held a purse and a stack of folders.

Florian explored the house, calling, "Hello?" until they heard voices coming from the backyard.

"Hey," Florian said, opening the backdoor and greeting the realtor and a pair of strangers chatting with her. "I didn't realize you were back here . . ."

Florian's eyes fixed on a point between the trees beyond their heads and forgot what they'd meant to say next. A gentle, moving glow wove between the trees and emerged from the forest.

"Mom?"

"Ah, you made it!" Cora called. "How lovely to see you, honey. And you must be the Pickerings. A pleasure." She crossed the yard with hardly a noticeable step, seemingly flowing from one point to another. She reached out and shook their hands in turn.

Without an explanation for her surprise appearance, she took a ballpoint pen and accepted the paperwork from the realtor whose mouth remained even more agape than Florian's.

"Mom?" they asked again, this time with less wonder and more growing frustration.

"Just a minute, honey, I need to sign these," she said without looking up, oblivious to her child's tone.

Florian fumed and pivoted, heading back into the house, but paused when their mom called to them to wait. She said a hasty farewell to the others and followed Florian out to their car.

"Florian, wait, honey."

"Why? I drove all the way out here when my to-do list is — why are you laughing at me?"

Cora chuckled. "I'm not laughing sweetheart, I just forgot how beautiful you are, my sweet baby."

"I'm almost thirty, Mom." Florian reminded her. "I have to get back. Glory's —"

Cora opened the passenger door and slid into the seat. Florian bent down and asked, "What are you doing?"

"Riding with you. I only just returned from my trip and don't have my car with me," Cora explained. "You can give your mother a ride, can't you? I'll buy you and Glory dinner and help with whatever you need."

Florian remained silent and started the engine. It took several minutes for everything to settle in their mind, and they started asking questions. "Where did you go on your trip? Why were you in the woods behind the house? Why didn't you come in through the front door?"

Their mother turned and stared at them, a huge smile on her face. "I visited a cloud forest with a friend."

"A cloud forest?" Florian asked skeptically. "Is this another one of your stories?"

"Hush, Child. It's in Costa Rica. Bumped into your amma while there, too."

"Maa's in Costa Rica right now?" Florian hadn't been checking their emails regularly. It was possible they missed a message about another research trip.

Cora hummed a few bars of a strange lullaby they'd never heard before and stared out the window. "I forgot how beautiful she is, too. We spent such a lovely time together catching up."

"I'm glad you two are able to get along after the divorce; it'll make holidays easier." Florian hedged a laugh but couldn't shake the feeling something was off. "Did you get hurt on your trip? Are you forgetting a lot these days, Mom?"

"Hm?" Cora asked, pulling her attention away from the window. "Oh no, I'm fine. It's just been so long since . . . well, traveling changes one's perspective, you know?"

Florian grumbled. "No, can't say that I do. I haven't been able to travel since I was a kid."

"That could change now," Cora said. "You only need to say

yes, and I can take you with me, and you'll have a lot more money soon."

"I can't take your money, Mom. You should use it to travel; you certainly seem happier than I've seen you in a while," Florian admitted. "Besides, with the shop opening soon, I'll be too busy for vacations for the foreseeable future."

Cora shook her head. "Oh, I won't need money for what I'm planning."

Florian laughed. "Good one. Who doesn't need money to fly off to Costa Rica and Australia and, uh, where else were you before that?"

"Japan," Cora answered. "The money will be yours eventually; I might as well give it all to you early."

Florian's eyes blurred red from the taillights in front of them. "Mom, I . . . don't talk like that, okay?"

They rode in silence the rest of the way. When they arrived at the soon-to-be shop, Glory stopped halfway in her greeting. "Miss Cora? Wow. When did you return? Where did you get those clothes? They're gorgeous and so strange!"

Florian only just noticed how oddly dressed Cora was. She always liked wearing bold colors and had a sense for fashion, but she stood draped in layers of delicate, multicolored fabric, each folded and tucked until it wove a pattern around her, somewhere between a dress and a jumpsuit, with the look of cape sleeves. Her hair had been woven in an equally complex plait and fastened with a silver clasp. She wore a stone pendant around her neck that appeared ordinary at first glance but glimmered in the corner of their eye when Florian looked away.

"Did you find that in Costa Rica?" Florian asked.

Cora shook her head and said, "It was a gift, long before Costa Rica. What needs to be done first?"

Glory, unaware of how strange Cora was behaving, replied, "The primer dried a few hours ago. We were going to start painting before the realtor called."

"Excellent. Let's paint, then."

"Oh, Miss Cora, you can't wear that lovely, um, dress, while painting," Glory said.

Cora laughed. "Nonsense! What color did you choose for the walls?"

Florian stood still watching their mother open a can of paint and prep her tools, wondering where she'd really gone and why she kept implying she'd been gone much longer than she had. Her eyes sparkled, and she radiated joy, as though she had healed all her past trauma in a few months and found the Fountain of Youth along the way.

"Are you going to make your old mother and gorgeous girl-friend do all the work?" Cora asked them.

Florian shook their head and rolled up their sleeves.

They painted the front room. Cora moved with an alacrity she never possessed in all the years Florian could remember, and she didn't flag or tire as she used to. They ate takeout from the taco truck at the corner, and during dessert Cora took it upon herself to start painting the crown molding, then slipped off to the bathroom for a while.

When Glory started yawning, Florian decided to pack it in. They could start stocking shelves and arranging chairs in the morning, once the paint dried. Fans whirred, drawing paint fumes out the windows, but they'd need to close the front and back doors and lock up soon. Cora had yet to return from the bath-room and Florian, worried, knocked on the door.

"Mom? Are you okay in there?" A small murmur in reply deepened their concern. "I'm coming in."

Cora crouched on the floor with a palette of paints Glory purchased in case they decided to use the stencils she'd bought. The whole wall across from the toilet bloomed with life — uncoiling fern fronds, flowering vines, and hidden mushrooms made from tiny brush strokes.

Florian worked their jaw but couldn't find their voice. Since when did their mom paint? Up until her recent trips, she had worked for decades as a bookkeeper, and the most creativity she displayed was through her wardrobe. "This is what you've been doing?"

"Mm-hmm. Do you like it?" Cora asked, still focused on shaping the shining carapace of a beetle amongst the green.

"Yeah," Florian breathed, a slight laugh coming to their throat. "It's wonderful. But Glory is getting tired. It's time to call it a night. Do you need a ride home?"

Cora finished the beetle and set down the brush. "No, thank you. Let me wash the brushes and we can go."

With the lights off and the doors locked, Cora kissed Florian's cheek and patted Glory's shoulder. "See you in the morning," she said, turning west on foot.

"Mom, where are you going? Your apartment is north of here. Are you sure you don't need a ride?" Florian asked.

Cora paused and smiled at her child. "No, honey. I didn't renew the lease. I won't be staying there tonight."

"What?! Well, are you staying at a hotel nearby or . . . ?" Florian knew the nearest hotel was at least three miles away.

"No, honey. I don't need a hotel. Good night." Cora turned left at the corner.

Florian and Glory shared a look. "We should follow her," Glory confirmed.

They jumped into the car and did a U-turn on the empty street, following Cora's path, which led to an elementary school's playground surrounded by trees, but when they looked for her, she had disappeared.

The next day, they found Cora sitting in a picnic chair outside the shop waiting for them. She refused to answer where she had gone or where she spent the night, but she appeared refreshed and in an entirely new outfit, equally as colorful and unusual in its design.

She worked from morning to evening, only pausing for food and bathroom breaks, and encouraging Florian and Glory to stretch when they flagged. By the time they were ready for rest, the shelves were stocked with books, comics, and games, and the tea counter held a few dozen tea varieties in hand-labeled glass jars.

Florian watched their mom turn left at the corner once more, and on the final day of preparation, appeared just as bright, eager, and energetic at the front door. They completed the front window display, placed the final decor pieces, set up a children's nook, and Florian's mom hung the Pride flag in the window for everyone to see.

In the afternoon, a journalist from the local paper came to interview the couple. Cora made a pot of tea for them.

Florian's nerves were shot, but the store was ready, and it looked better than they hoped. Glory gave their sweaty hand a squeeze while they answered questions. When the interviewer left, Florian went to thank their mom for all the help, but she appeared to have slipped out the back, leaving only a note on the counter:

Thank you for letting me be a part of your shop's creation. I must leave again; there is much to see in this huge world and little time left to see it. Good luck on the grand opening!

Florian handed Glory the note and leaned heavily on the counter, unable to fight back the tears. "She's gone again."

"What's your name, little human?" asked a lilting voice from behind a tree.

A small child, bending down to retrieve her ball, froze in place at the unexpected voice. With a hesitant glance up, she saw a lilac-toned face peering back at her. "C-Cora."

The strange person tittered with delight. "It's not wise to tell a fairy your name," they said.

Her hands fastened on her ball and eyes widened with wonder. "Are you a fairy?"

"As sure as you're a human child," they assured her. "Do not worry, I promise not to use your name against you. Would you like to see something delightful?"

Cora nodded, curls bouncing with her excitement.

"Then take my hand and come away with me. There is much to show you," they said.

She shook her head. "Oh, no. I'm not supposed to go with strangers."

"Hm," the fairy said, squatting down to meet Cora eye-to-eye. "Very well. We will stay here and play, and I will show you what I can at the edge of the woods. Is that agreeable?"

Cora screwed up her face as she considering it, then offered a decisive nod.

"Wonderful! First, you should take this. It will help you see what's been hidden." The fairy opened their slender fingers revealing a doughnut-shaped stone. "Keep it close, and when you want to find me, hold it up to your eye."

The fairy disappeared from her sight, but Cora lifted the stone and looked through it, one brown eye peering through to the fairy's shining yellow eyes. "Peekaboo, I see you!"

The fairy laughed. "Very good! Now are you ready to play?"

"Mm-hmm." Cora beamed up at the fairy. "What's your name?"

The fairy took her hand and laughed. "Can you keep a secret?"

"Yes."

"It is only fair you have the same power over me that I hold over you, since you so willingly shared your name, but you mustn't tell anyone else. Not ever. Do you understand?"

"Yes! I promise!" Cora assured them.

The fairy's smile widened with approval. "Treyva."

"Trey-va," Cora said quietly to herself.

"Correct. Now what would you like to play?"

Mrs. Thompson swept the broken glass around the entryway and dumped it into a paper bag while a handful of customers and friends continued tidying the books that had been knocked down.

"Thank you, Mrs. Thompson. I appreciate the help," Florian said, holding an ice pack to their cheek.

"It's not a problem. How are you?" she asked.

Florian pulled away the ice to show her. "The cut was small, and the swelling's gone down. No need to worry."

"That bruise is going to be noticeable for a while, but that's not what concerns me. How are you and Glory holding up?"

Florian motioned for the neighbor to have a seat at the table. "I'll be fine, but Glory's pretty shaken up. It's the third attack since our opening, and this one . . ."

"Hurt people," Mrs. Thompson finished for them. "Sometimes people stop at nasty words, but others continue to escalate. Did you order those cameras I recommended?"

Florian shook their head. "Glory's ordering them now."

Their neighbor pursed her lips, but didn't admonish them. "I'll check my cameras to see if I can give you a clear picture to give to the police."

"Thank you," Florian said, standing up. "Folks, I'm grateful for your help, but for safety's sake, I need to ask you all to leave for the day. We'll be closing up shop until we can repair the window and ensure your future safety."

A few disappointed murmurs went around the small group. One of the customers said, "Let me grab some wood from my workshop; I can at least help you board the windows until you can get new glass installed."

"Thanks, Jeremy; I appreciate that."

Glory came out from the back room and offered everyone a gift card for future purchases and handed out to-go cups to those who hadn't finished their tea.

When the last person left, Glory's cheeks and nose turned red.

Florian caught her before she crumpled and guided her to the loveseat against the wall. "It's going to be okay, Glory. We'll get new glass and install cameras. This isn't our first rodeo with these clowns."

Glory kept crying, unable to speak, and Florian held her tight, worried that maybe Mrs. Thompson was right. What if next time they did more? Will they come in and hurt people directly? Commit arson? Bring guns? The town used to be more tolerant, but it felt like the thin veneer of pretense had washed away in recent years.

Before Florian could say anything further, their phone rang. They glanced at the screen in case it was the police or the contractor, but it was neither.

They answered the call. "Hello, Maa."

"Florian! I need you to come to Monteverde right away. I'll buy the tickets if you need, but you must —"

"Maa, what's wrong?" Florian straightened and Glory quieted, listening closely to the conversation. Florian put the phone on speaker.

"It's Cora," Navi replied. "She's saying the most bizarre things."

"You found Mom?! Where did you say you are?" Florian asked. It had been over six months since she'd disappeared, and now Maa said they were together? Florian's mind whirled with confusion, fear, anger . . . hurt. "I can't just drop my life and, and —"

"Florian Lughani, you will march on that plane tonight and help me, or —"

"Or what?" Florian demanded.

Navi's voice hitched. Florian recognized the sound of their Maa crying. "We might lose her. Forever."

Florian, left speechless by this, caught Glory's determined look.

"Book two tickets, Miss Navi," Glory said. "We're both coming." She whispered to Florian, "I'll text Amanda and ask her to handle things. We'll pay her time and half for the extra help."

"Glory," Florian said in a low voice, "you don't have to —"

"Oh, yes, I do," Glory said. "We're partners, right?"

"Yes, of course, but —"

"But nothing." She spoke louder so Navi could hear. "We need to pack, but we can be at the airport in two hours."

Although the humid air made every breath feel heavy and skin bead with sweat, Cora remained in a state of excitement on the edge of euphoria. In her time traveling the forests across four continents, seeing the wonders beyond the view of most humans and learning how to influence the world with the skills Treyva taught her, trivial matters like humidity, sore joints, and grief no longer troubled her.

She crossed the threshold between Treyva's realm and the forest where Navi currently conducted her research. The air tasted of rain and tropical blooms, and this forest lacked the mossy paths that wound around the realm of the fairies. Reconnecting with Navi had been worth the distraction from her studies.

Navi waited for her at one of the suspension bridges, her eyes searching back and forth through the trees for signs of her. Cora smiled and emerged to Navi's left when she glanced right and surprised her. "Oh! Cora! Must you startle me like that?"

"I'm sorry, Navi. I didn't realize I needed to announce myself," she said, while her hand idly stroked the stem of an orchid.

Navi laughed. "How did you learn to walk so silently?"

"Did I used to stomp like an elephant? I've forgotten." Cora closed the distance. "What did you want to show me today?"

Navi studied her ex-wife's glowing face, the sparkle of her eyes, and did not recognize her. "We must wait a little while longer; someone is joining us."

Cora took a step back. "Who?"

But Navi didn't need to answer. On the other side of the bridge two people held fast to the rails, the shorter of the two in a crouch, appearing ill.

Glory paused and turned back, giving Florian a hand, but their progress across the bridge was slow. Every time it swayed, Florian cried out in alarm and shut their eyes.

When at last they reached the end and stepped off the bridge, Florian squatted down and gasped for air. "I . . . am not . . . crossing . . . that bridge . . . again."

"You'll have to if you want to go home," Navi informed them.

Florian glanced up, their forehead covered in a sheen of sweat. "Then I live here now," they replied, plopping down on the ground. "Hello, mothers mine."

Navi hugged Glory in greeting, while Cora squatted to greet Florian.

"Are you my surprise?" Cora asked, brushing strands of hair from her child's face. "What a delight to see you again. I had forgotten how beautiful you are."

"Mo-om," Florian complained, as though they were still a teen. "Quit it. What do you mean you forgot? You said that the last time you came to visit me. What are you even doing here?" Florian stood, dusting leaves from their pants.

Cora refused to answer the question but waited smiling to see their child again. "What a lovely diversion you are."

"Diversion from what, Miss Cora?" Glory asked.

Navi said, "Follow me. There's a small clearing of sorts not far from here. We can sit and talk there."

Cora followed Navi, and the younger couple followed behind whispering between them. "Is this treat your doing, Navi? Did you bring them here so I could say goodbye?"

This time Navi refused to answer. She set down her pack between a sparse stand of short trees with broad leaves and offered snacks between them. Florian took a swig from their water bottle but remained standing.

Cora studied their face, their posture, feeling the minutes slip by and the urgency to leave grow stronger, but Florian had come all this way to see her, surely the work could wait a while longer. Her fingers sketched symbols in the air at her sides, practicing during silent moments. Treyva whispered in her ear that they would need to leave when the sun dipped another ten degrees lower.

"How is the shop? Does everyone love the tea?" Cora asked her child.

"No, it's not fine. Some bigots tossed bricks through the windows yesterday. We ought to be cleaning up, installing cameras, and instead we're here because Maa said you're leaving? That we might not see you again. What's going on?"

Cora focused on Florian and noticed the bandage across a swollen, purple-brown cheek. She pushed Treyva's insistent reminders from her mind and really saw her family. "Oh, no, honey. I'm so sorry. I . . . thought you had come to see me off." Cora lowered her head.

Florian grabbed her by the arms. "What are you talking about? See you off where? Ever since your parents died you haven't been yourself. You're . . . you're scaring me!"

The hold on her arms turned painful, but Cora didn't show discomfort. Her eyes to Florian's, seeing her sweet child in so much pain. "I'm so sorry, honey. I have to go. They need me. There's so much to do and time is slipping away from us."

"*I* need you, Mom. I need you. I don't know what you think is more important out here in the forest, but I've spent my whole life with one mother always running away; I don't think I can take losing you both."

Navi walked up behind Florian and placed a hand on their shoulder. "Is that how you feel, beta?"

Cora's heart constricted, caught between the despair in her child's eyes and the pull of the fairy realm. "I would love to stay with you, honey, but they're calling me to go. The sun will pass overhead soon, and —"

"Who?" Florian demanded. "Who is calling you? You're hearing voices now? We can get you help. Come back with us, come home and we'll find someone to figure this out."

Cora shook her arms free of Florian's hold and slipped her hands in theirs. "Here, my child, take this and it might help you see."

Florian huffed in frustration. "Fine," they whispered.

Florian studied the stone pendant in their hand. "Is this from that box I found in the attic?"

"Yes, honey. Hold it up to your eye and look through," Cora gently instructed.

"I —" Florian stopped their protest and sighed, lifting the stone up to their right eye. Through the stone, the world appeared brighter, more verdant. Paths of dancing lights wove between the trees and their mom appeared to glow with an inner light. And next to her . . .

Florian lowered and raised the stone. An odd, slender person stood near Cora. "Mom? Who is that?"

Cora smiled. "May I tell them?"

The figure appeared to all of them, folding their arms and huffing once more. "You promised."

"I will not share your name," Cora affirmed. "Family, this is an old friend. A fairy I met behind my house when I was very young."

Neither Navi nor Florian could speak, but Glory took a step forward and offered her hand to the fairy. "Hello, I'm —"

"Do not give them your name," Cora warned, and Glory caught herself.

"A pleasure to make your acquaintance. I've never met a fairy before," Glory said.

Treyva smiled and took her hand. "Well, are you not charming?" They chuckled and placed a hand on Cora's shoulder. "I am happy, for Cora's sake, she could see you all before we return to work."

"Why does she have to leave?" Florian asked. "What hold do you have on her?"

Treyva gawped, offended. "I have no hold on her; she chooses to take on this task."

Glory linked her arm with Florian's. "What task?"

Treyva studied them all, looked to Cora, and decided to share the details. "The fairy realm is dying. For two generations now, we have sought out humans open to our skills to aid us in holding on to what remains, and we hope, in time, our numbers will increase again."

"What do humans have to do to help?" Florian asked.

Treyva frowned. "There is much to say and little time to say it."

"Why?" Florian demanded. "What is so urgent that *one* human cannot be absent for so short a period?"

"Time moves differently in my realm, and . . . ah!" Treyva threw up their hands and turned away.

Cora smiled sadly. "I need to go. Come with me, Florian. You could all come to the fairy realm and then we would never need to say goodbye."

"We can't just leave our lives! Maa's research? Our store? We have lives to live here, and so do you."

Cora covered a cry of pain and shook her head, but Florian wouldn't let their mother go so easily. They walked around her to face the stubborn fairy, somehow shorter than Florian themself.

"Fairy," Florian said in a soft voice. "Is there no way my mother can help you and still be with her family? Why can't we stay together in our world *and* work to save yours?"

Treyva opened and shut their mouth. "Hm. I will pose this question to the others and return."

Children ran by Tea and Treasures shouting at one another, somehow managing to avoid Cora, who was only a few brush strokes away from completing the frame around the window. Although the humans who passed by could not see it, each stroke was imbued with magic, both for protection and attraction. Those sensitive to magic would intuitively be drawn in.

Florian came out to inspect the work and held up the stone to see the glowing symbols coursing through the art. "Beautiful, Mom. Just beautiful."

"You won't need that soon," Cora said. "Keep practicing, honey."

"Is that what your fairy says?" Florian asked.

"Why don't you ask them?" Cora replied.

In the empty back lot behind the row of stores, a row of saplings stood ready for planting now that the community had claimed it from the city and cleared it of debris. Navi's efforts to replenish the soil were evident in the rich black of the earth. Soon the community garden would boast an orchard and garden reaching all the way to the woods around the elementary school.

Though only visible to Cora's family, Treyva watched approvingly as they planted the first tree in the hole.

"What do you think, old friend?" Cora whispered. "Will this be a start?"

Treyva crouched down and touched the young roots of the sapling. "She will grow strong and well and connect with our boundaries. Yes, this is a better start than we could have hoped for."

A child ran up to help stomp the soil down around the sapling's roots, but paused, wide-eyed and looked up into smiling yellow eyes.

"Hello, child," Treyva said.

"He can see you?" Cora asked.

"Oh, yes. Yes, he can." Treyva's smile broadened.

ABOUT RAVEN J. DEMERS

Raven J. Demers writes speculative fiction and is the author of Perdition and The Corvid and the Calico and co-author of the Amakai series. Xe earned a B.A. in Anthropology from the University of Washington and is a member of the Northwest Independent Writers Association. Raven lives in a forest near Seattle, WA with xyr family and believes the answer to xyr farming obsession might be ducks. More information can be found at: satyrsgarden.com or @neversremedy on Twitter

WE NEED PRETTY THINGS

S.M. FOX

*S*he was so beautiful at that moment. A sparkler in the cosmos. The flaming tin can that coursed through the sea of endless stars still had gravity detection. The pilot was powerless to stop the ship from being guided toward the nearest land mass large enough to have its own orbit. That was the goal of this mission. The life of the pilot was not a priority — or even expected. These ships flew for hundreds of years, after all.

The pilot thrashed and slammed her fists on the console of blinking buttons. She roared in defiance as the heat of the malfunctioning ship melted her seatbelt buckle. Melting plastic smoked within the cabin. They never told her that if something went wrong, the ship would seek a planet, any planet, and fling itself into the atmosphere.

She expected to die on the ship, just not like this.

The academy she attended was more like a crash course. They geared every lecture toward protecting the pods. Though her professors never explicitly said it, the pilot felt the intent like a whisper in her ear.

You're all going to die up there, but staying isn't an option anymore.

The mask on the pilot's face released something other than

oxygen. They did not cover it in class, but she got the sense that she was being drugged. A merciful act if the mass-produced ships could not endure the unknown. She waved her gloved hands in front of her mask. Like comets she could control, they had their own wispy tails.

She was a Valkyrie.

Responsible for ushering the children to their deaths before they had been born. A shot in the dark, raging against a void that never cared. A humanity that might survive, though no one truly expected it. This was better than roasting alive back home. Her neck went soft like the protein packs she had been eating for the last nine years and the pilot found herself back at the academy.

#

Someone had lice.

Thom was scratching his head on the bunk next to hers. She thought nothing of it until the newest recruit on the top bunk also began scratching. It wasn't long before she too shivered as tiny legs skittered around the nape of her neck. The newest recruit in the top bunk belonged in elementary school. A girl about the age of ten and her hair had been unbrushed for years.

Guilt was a gnawing thing, not unlike the pincers that clung to her scalp. She could have offered to help the kid. At least cut the mats out. But she just couldn't bring herself to do anything these days.

The solution came at the hand of a senior officer and a pair of clippers. Everyone was required to shave their heads. She told herself that her hair didn't matter. They were all about to be launched into space anyway. Pride and identity were nothing in the face of certain death, and yet her eyes watered as the clippers glided over her skin.

She restrained a sniffle when chunks of white-blonde hair fell into her lap. Her father was always so proud of their heritage. They were descendants of the old gods, from a time where mortals did not fear death. Where women were beautiful and wicked. Not the unassuming, docile pets of men.

The pilot did not feel strong in her bunk that night. She cried over her hair. It was petty and useless, but it was the last scrap of her identity, of who she was before the seas boiled and the rocks became too hot to pick from the shore.

"Your hair was really pretty," a small voice came from the upper bunk. "I'm sorry."

Tears rolled down her temples, and she sniffed. "It's not important."

"But it was still pretty," she said. "We need pretty things no matter what happens next."

The girl must have felt she was to blame, but she was glad they shaved her head. Now the neglected little girl had a sense of anonymity among the ranks. They were all orphans, but some had been alone for too long.

Rolling over, the pilot fished through the bag under her bunk and found what she was searching for. The echoes of ocean water and grit of sand sent her back to the shores. This was the closest the kid would ever come to an ocean. At least she could share the last bit of joy she held dear.

"Here," she said, reaching up through the bars.

A small hand clasped hers before finding the object. The kid gasped. "What is it?"

"It's a clam shell. My father and I used to collect them before things got bad."

"You're giving this to me?"

The pilot had stopped crying. The rushing sounds of the shore came to greet her. The smell of damp and seaweed and the clacking of seagulls. Her father's smile was her own at that moment. The bleakness of their situation could not take everything.

"Yes," she said. "Because pretty things matter."

She was smiling when she closed her eyes to go to sleep. As the bed tilted upright, the blanket fell away. The pilot didn't want to open her eyes, but the beeping was loud and insistent. The room around her jerked and heaved, and she wondered when the bunks came with seat belts.

The heat was unbearable. She tried to wipe the sweat that had accumulated around her mouth and nose, only to find something strapped to her face. The pilot opened her eyes, and it all came hurtling back. She was not at the academy. She was on a crashing ship destined for a planet, regardless of its viability.

The drugs were not helping.

She tore off the mask. Burning, metallic air greeted her lungs. The electricity in the cabin was high. How long had it been breaking down? The academy taught them to keep the mask on as often as possible and now the pilot understood why. The smell of melted wires would create an unnecessary panic.

Reading the ship manuals wasn't required, but the pilot had. They equipped each spacecraft with one. It was a long time in space, and she had lots of time to read. Nowhere in the manual did it mention a distress beacon, but there was a seatbelt cutter. That was when she realized the truth of it all.

She broke the cutter free from its plastic mount and sawed away at the belt. She was no spacecraft engineer, but she knew a thing or two about wiring. Had the world not gone to total shit, she would have taken up her father's craft.

The ship jerked, and the pilot gripped the arms of the chair for stability. The light show on her dashboard gave little indication as to what was wrong, but the biggest of the lights was green and no longer glowing. The pods.

The pilot staggered toward the back of the cabin. She had to override the door, but the ship still responded to her as the captain and accepted the code she punched into the keypad. There was technically nothing wrong with the engine. The ship could have continued its journey, but if something compromised the pods, the ship would crash land on the nearest planet before the contents died.

If the pilot could restore the pods, the ship would stabilize.

She tried to run through the narrow galley that comprised her living quarters. The bed was built into the wall. A series of compartments that stowed her protein packs. The booth and table melded into the wall. When she first boarded, it reminded her of the RV she and her father had been remodeling.

"Why is everything latched and stuck to the walls?" she had asked.

Her father, with his great fluffy beard and bright blue eyes, smiled and patted the kitchenette. "So we can drive without all our things flying about the place."

The ship jutted again, and she crashed into a cabinet. Nothing fell out of place, no matter how throttled they were. The next door led to the pod incubators. She punched in her keycode, but it refused to answer. An angry red bulb flashed in response. She had no access to this room.

An automated voice sounded through the speaker. "Retinal scan required."

They were told at the academy that they could not enter the room. A pilot might contaminate the delicate biological matter stored within the pods. The ship would land on a planet and release the pods. It would take decades before they would yield results, but that was all a part of the plan.

The sole purpose of the pilot was to send communications back home. Voices echoing through the cosmos, hoping others would arrive decades later. But only the most viable planets would win settlers. The planet she was hurtling towards was a gray, rocky mass. Not a promising settlement, especially not if she were dead.

Slamming her palm against the keypad, she cursed it. There was something wrong inside the room. A shortage or maybe just a faulty sensor. She needed to get in there and fix it before the ship crashed, taking her with.

"Computer," she called out. "Is there another way to access pod storage?"

"Retinal scan required."

The pilot searched the galley for anything to pry the door open. She had read somewhere in the manual that the interior came apart easily. That way, when the ship landed, the pilot could construct a shelter. They equipped it with basic tools built within the panels.

Ripping off her gloves, her fingernails searched the seams assembled along the galley. When they caught, she pulled, revealing a compartment with a variety of tools. There was no crowbar, but there was an ax. She yanked it off the rack and began swinging at the door. Big, rounded swings like her father taught her.

The doors didn't splinter the way firewood did. The aluminum dented and clanged as her strikes began to lose their momentum. She had been in space for nine years. Muscle and bone deteriorated in space. Her labored breaths were a reminder that she had not kept up with her exercises.

A shudder ran through the galley. The floor beneath her was a roiling sea. Her feet slipped out from underneath her as she waved her arms about, searching for anything just to stay afloat. A crack reverberated down her spine and between her ears. An intense nausea erupted from her belly. The pilot rolled over and puked.

She had been staring at the stars for the last nine years. An unnecessary feature but one implemented by the design team by that Uber-rich guy funding the program. The pilot thought she had seen every kind of star, — bright, pale, red, and falling — but none compared to the black stars that stole her vision before she fainted.

The soft slip of plastic against plastic, and she faced a binder. Its edges did not fray. They curled from the countless fingers that turned the pages before her.

Sitting on an unyielding chair, she was a daughter for the last time.

"These are the only caskets available for rent, I'm afraid." The man with a forgettable face and a soft voice pointed at two near-identical coffins. "With the resource shortage and the rate of...loss, we're reduced to renting them. We also have a table. If you can't afford to rent..."

She would have welcomed sadness. Or anything. Had the declining world around her stripped her of all emotion? The pangs of loss that punched through her heart when Mama died still ached to this day, but it was a different time then.

And it wasn't for Mama that she grieved. It was a grief for all the things she wanted but would never have. She couldn't picture her mother's face, but they shared the same pale-white locks. Father was different. He was her whole world, a shining beacon in the storm. When his light went out, emptiness swallowed her whole.

According to her father, only Ginnungagap existed before Odin and his brothers killed Ymir and created the universe. It was a bleak, eternal void. It never occurred to her that Ginnungagap resided within her ribcage.

She slid the binder back at him. "There won't be a funeral, just cremate him."

The forgettable man was staring at her then. His eyes prodded for her to look at him. It was the polite thing to do, but she lacked the energy to follow along. What did a hollow drum care when played?

"You're all that's left?"

She nodded.

"I know some people," he suggested. "They will claim you're their child. I'll say you ran away..."

The forgettable man's lines were rehearsed and precise. She didn't doubt his intentions. There were groups that did indeed seek to rescue orphans from the space mission critics called "Flip's last Flop."

"What does it matter how I die?" Bile pooled in the back of her throat. "In space or covered in tumors like my father?"

As soon as it came, the bitterness was gone. Replaced by the numbness. Maybe it was just her way. An empty journal like the ones she carried around in school. She only wanted one because all her friends had them. They poured their secrets into those journals and shared them with only those closest to them.

A boy in their class would steal them and read the embarrassing contents out loud while the girls shrieked like harpies. One day, he stole hers.

He jumped out of reach and tore the journal open, then looked at her in astonishment. "There's nothing in here."

She had nothing to say. There were no deep-harbored loves or cherished secrets. When the moles on her father's hands spread, she felt the same. Nothing. If anyone deserved to be launched into space on a one-way trip, it was her.

Forty-eight hours was the time they gave her before reporting to the academy. Enough time to say goodbye to friends if they were still alive and to pack bags she didn't need.

Armed with a bag full of seashells and underwear. The government confiscated anything of value to help fund the "Children of the Stars" project. The government would melt and strip all resources of the coastal property. They may have used the gold from her parents' wedding rings for the spacecraft she would die in.

Anything for the cause.

She stood on her porch and looked out onto the ocean, now too hot to touch. How she longed to wade in the salty waters of her youth, but the salt was long gone as was the seaweed and the creatures in the tidepools. There were no more seashells to collect, and there was no more Father to collect them with.

\#

The academy was little more than an intake port. She went from one line to another for what seemed like a day before they led her to a squeaky plastic seat. One among many, she faced a stage where a man in a military uniform would brief them.

He beamed with a fervent pride or perhaps he was nervous. It was hard to tell. Why would he be smiling at a time like this? No one smiled back. They had all lost too much and had forgotten how.

"Y'all are in for a real treat." The badges pinned to his uniform glared in the spotlight. "The man who started it all, our visionary, is here to give you the presentation!"

His excitement plunked like a rock in the ocean. He impressed no one. They must have been just as empty as she was. All around her were kids who had lost everything. Each with their own story that would sound oh so like her own.

As stiffly pressed as his uniform was, she couldn't help but notice the pit stains forming and the gleam of sweat along his short-clipped hair. It was hot in the room, but the thrum of the air conditioning did not come on until Philip Rusk jaunted on the stage.

He smiled and waved as if he were expecting applause, but there was none. The speakers hanging from the ceiling trumpeted patriotic music. Some children were so startled they cried. Others flinched and ducked as if expecting something to fall on them. Sweat poured down the officer's face in shiny lines, but Philip Rusk appeared totally unaware.

"Look at you," he said with an air of bewilderment. "My children of the stars. You are our future."

He enunciated each word as if he truly meant it, but she knew the truth. He cared more about his vision than he did for anyone in that room. His legacy. The fleeting bleat of humanity before it snuffed itself out, taking its brief but horrid history into the void where her heart lay.

"Here, we will train you in the basics. Survival, emergency protocols, and what to do when you land your very own ship. You are the masters of your fate as well as ours. You are the ones who will land our pods on new planets where they will create habitable atmospheres. Inside each pod are the building blocks to recreate a world like our own."

He paused for dramatic effect. Failing to read the room, he could not see that the children were tired. She was so very tired.

"When you land, a distress beacon will notify us of your success. Each ship has enough food and supplies to last you a lifetime. When you land, we will prioritize a rescue mission and take you home or come and join you!"

Did she detect a flicker of fear in his eyes? At any moment, they could all stand up and walk out. They could revolt and beat him to death with their plastic chairs and their small fists. The children in the room outnumbered the adults tenfold, yet they didn't move. Why didn't they move?

For some intangible reason, the man on the stage was the one in power and they, the masses, were not. His wealth was enough to rebuild a small settlement of people and enough shields from the radiation to raise healthy adults, yet they sent children to space before the tumors grew.

Yet, it was their stolen money that funded the launch, not his. All the while, he smiled at them like they were lambs for the slaughter because he *knew*. He knew they would never stand up.

"The most brilliant part of my design is that we will have our pick of a new home. We get to decide the ideal place to live, and this time we won't destroy it for resources. Each of you represents a planet full of resources and a viable atmosphere ripe for the picking. Never again will our children know this pain, and it's all thanks to you."

Something thrummed in the space her heart once lived. They were the last remaining resource at his disposal. If they failed, that was it. Why was the end of humanity such a bad thing?

"You know why I picked orphans as my Children of the Stars?"

Because they were powerless? A large mass of people without a voice.

He leaned into the podium as if he were telling them a secret. "Because orphans are always searching for home."

\#

The pilot's senses were returning. Reality was slowly returning to her prone body. The rancid smell of regurgitated protein packs and iron came first. There were few smells in a spacecraft, even one on fire. She moved her head and noted the slick floor her face was laying in. Opening her eyes, the pilot found she was lying in a pile of vomit and blood. It was a wonder she woke up at all.

She was grateful for the suit designed to eliminate bodily waste. Philip Rusk gave them that small comfort at least. The world spun a little as she propped herself up on a bruised elbow. The keypad sparked and hung by frayed wires. Though the ax had failed to open the pod room, the jolt that knocked her unconscious had damaged the security system.

Pulling herself to her feet, the pilot picked up the ax. Her head spun when she bent over, and she leaned against the wall for a long moment before resuming. "Computer," she gasped. "I need access to pod storage."

"Retinal scanner damaged. Cannot locate administrator. Attempting to use the scanner may result in blindness."

She laughed at her luck. "Computer, who is administrator?"

The computer's voice warped and varied in volume. "Administrator unknown."

That confirmed it. With the administrator data lost, any retinal scan would do, but entering the atmosphere compromised the system. What protected the retina from the intense lasers no longer functioned, but going blind in one eye was a sacrifice she would make.

The pilot pressed against the wall. "Computer, retinal scan."

"Warning—"

"Computer, override!"

The pilot expected pain, but there was none. Just a bright flash and then nothing. She blinked several times just to be sure, but her vision was completely gone in one eye. Before she could think more on it, the doors before her slid open.

She stepped in just before the room sealed itself. The metal groaned with finality before the floor fell away with each step. She wasn't walking at all. She was floating. Weightless, she arched her back and let herself float adrift in the sea of green eggs that almost reminded her of sea turtles.

Her life had been just one everyday tragedy after another. An orphan ejected from her dying planet not for hope, but for the sake of a greedy man searching the cosmos for more plunder. So many years she laid awake at night wondering if pain was real.

Rocked by a highly-controlled gravity, the tears left her eyes and glimmered like diamonds.

"Thank you," she whispered.

Insulated and protected in an indestructible room, the turmoil outside became a distant thing. The crash landing did not disturb them. It had been a mechanical failure, after all. The pods and the stasis were performing in optimal range. It wasn't until the buzzing became a soft humming that gravity slowly returned to the room. She lazily drifted to the floor first. Then the pods came sinking down all around her.

The fire was out long before the doors opened.

Little had survived the wreckage, but her space suit with its limited supply of air had. Pulling the helmet over her blood-matted head, she noticed that the pods were already going to work. Some had burst into clouds of green smoke like puff mushrooms. Others opened in a series of spirals. Water poured from most of them, creating a pool on the floor.

The space suit was heavy. She had only taken a few steps from the dilapidated shuttle before she fell to her knees, gasping for limited air. The pilot turned to the pods again to see vines sprouting from the ash-colored terrain.

Could those pods create enough of an atmosphere before her oxygen support gave out? She thought that was just Flip Rusk bullshit, but on the ideal planet, the pods could thrive. The pilot didn't know what were lies and what was truth, but she reasoned that if money was the motivator, it was likely the truth.

Rather than exert her energy and waste her oxygen, the pilot lay flat on her back and practiced the shallow, meditative breathing they taught at the academy. She centered herself on a time when she was happiest. The ocean was lukewarm on her feet and the tides roared and pushed her back.

The sands were full of glass and microplastic, so she had to wear shoes, but there were still shells for her to find.

"Look here!"

She turned to find her father waving at her from the shore. He was pointing at something in the sand. Wading through the waters, weight returned to her legs as she met him. His eyes were the color of the long-lost icebergs against an ever orange sky.

"Look at this," he said.

It was a perfectly round shell with a star etched into it. She picked it up and investigated. "It's not man-made."

"No," her father said. "It's called a sand dollar."

Never had she felt such wonder. Nature had made this thing of its own accord. Its perfection was unaided by human design. It was real, and it smelled so wonderful. Like the ocean itself created one last masterpiece just for them.

She was happy then. Happy and sad. All the emotions came pouring in all at once, filling her like a tidepool. Life bloomed in tidepools, and she could be a safe harbor if she wanted. There was no distress beacon, and she had drifted for a long time. Far removed from the trajectory, humanity may never find her or her pods.

It could have been days or even weeks before she fully woke, but the screen on her helmet lit with a flashing red light to warn her that the oxygen supply was nearly gone.

Well Astrid, this is it.

Her fingers searched for the buttons along her helmet. A whooshing noise sounded, and daylight assaulted her eyes. She squinted and shielded her face before letting go of that last final breath.

What Astrid inhaled was life. It was an ashy, unsatisfying breath of air, but the pods were truly developing oxygen. She quickly learned that the oxygen had yet to branch far from their source, but each day she found herself able to walk a little farther and breathe a little deeper.

The vines were now rooted and reaching the sky as saplings developed their bark. Clone bees woke from hibernation and began pollinating the flowers. It was a small garden, and in the center was the beginnings of a massive tree.

She named it Yggdrasill. The ash tree that grew from the remains of a dead god. Philip Rusk was once a god to many, but his creations only served as fertilizer for the tree she tended to. It would suspend the heavens and support balance within the universe.

Joy was what she felt when she found the shore. Astrid cried and laughed before choking on the small supply of oxygen. There was an ocean. That was why the pods took to the ash soil. Everything the pods required was already there.

Her father told her about the end of days. Volcanoes erupting until there was nothing left. Perhaps that was what happened here. An entire ecosystem dormant and waiting for a breath of new life. Just like her.

The shore was a field of sharp rocks, but she found a cove. That was when she saw it.

Pressed into the sand was a shell.

Smooth and worn from time, but there were still ripples of life and the smooth, pearlescent colors were signs of life carved along the remaining ridges. She clutched the shell and held it close to her heart. Closing her eyes, she smiled.

ABOUT S.M. FOX

S.M Fox writes myth-based fantasies. Her Arthurian inspired novel, The Seven Wives of Octavian, will be available on Amazon in spring, 2023. Follow her on Twitter @SMFoxAuthor.

SCALES

EMMERYN PALLADINO

When the scales began to break through skin, they said you were becoming a monster. Blue and green, seafoam to pearl. You weren't certain at what point you started to believe them.

You began to wrap yourself in tighter layers, a futile effort to not draw attention to the rough patches. Elbows, knees, along your arms, mottled with foundation and concealer caked on like spackle. Toner to offset the iridescent shine so that a passing glance wouldn't be drawn to it. Constant checks and double checks, bathroom visits far beyond the routine.

Your careful camouflage is usually enough to deflect scrutiny, but occasionally a stranger catches on. Nobody has said anything to you yet, but you have noticed more glances on the train. The old woman's frown of disapproval. The young man with something to prove to you, himself, the world. His jaw tightens as he calculates his ability to start something. You tuck your chin and pretend to be busy with your phone. In the dark screen you can see the skin flaking on your cheeks. The beginnings of another patch betray you.

As you touch up in the bathroom mirror you tell yourself you wanted this, that you were prepared for the hardships.

You walk to the public library after your shift ends. You walk most places these days, telling yourself it's a last hurrah. The fact is you sold your car to make a dent in the cost. You'll sell everything eventually. You're going to have to.

The forums have a list of books everyone checks out when they choose this path. There aren't many, and most are fantasy. There's a running joke: if anyone mentions Hans Christen Anderson, run. You spot The Little Mermaid on a small display. You don't run. You check out the books. The librarian gives a knowing nod, but doesn't remark. You silently thank her for the discretion.

You take a long shower, makeup swirling down the drain. You can't help but scratch at the itchy patches on your thighs, peeling skin tearing away for new growth. Shampoo and blood circle under your feet. Your fingernails are sharper than they were this morning. You exfoliate, letting the city, public transit, glances of strangers be cleansed. Your reflection in the mirror — a colorful smattering of new scales dusting your cheeks — is tear-streaked, ethereal. *Beautiful.*

You knock the concealer into the trash bin.

Your mother left a voicemail. She avoids the elephant seal in the room, talks about her gardening, a cousin's new baby. She lingers for a moment, then: *You're being selfish.* She burns brightly as a beratement begins, emboldened. But without someone to riff with she loses steam, trails off and repeats it. *You're being shellfish.* She can't help it; she laughs despite herself. There's a minute where she doesn't speak, but you can tell she's waiting for the sob in the back of her throat to settle. She promises she'll come to your party, and the voicemail ends.

You still haven't heard from your father. You don't expect you will. You've made peace with that.

You do your weekly injection on the alternating leg, needle piercing deep into a gap between scales. The plunger delivers 200mg of concentrated hope directly into your bloodstream, salt water in salt water. You put a Hello Kitty Band-Aid over it and wait for the feeling of ice in your veins to settle, the tension to go out of your muscles. It doesn't.

There is an enraged man on the street, spit flying, a home-made sandwich board making his message clear: *The Siren Is The Devil's Agent.* The back offers an equally cogent argument: *Go Back To Atlantis, Fish Freaks.* You would if you could, you think dryly. He notices you and seethes, but the current of the crowd carries you away before he can curse you out.

You drag your potted plants down to the front stoop and post a craigslist ad: Free to a Good Home. They're gone within the hour. You allow yourself the rare indulgence of posting a selfie, eyes closed, serene, to the subreddit: *Learning to love my scales <3!* It's still difficult to type on your phone with the new claws. The upvotes start to come in; everyone loves a guppy.

You catch up on the shows you haven't gotten to yet. Where there was once only the metaphorical List, there is now an actual list. Despite your best efforts, it's becoming increasingly clear you're not going to finish all of them. You knock a few off, restructure the list based on length. It still looks too long.

You have dreams about choking on toxic waste, getting minced by a boat propeller. You keep a running count of the number of times you've dreamt of getting your head stuck in a six-pack of soda rings. You're up to four.

Every few days you do laps in the local pool. You're getting faster, but it feels exposed. There are whispers around the locker room.

Your cat knows something is happening but doesn't under-stand what that means for her. You hold her whenever and for as long as she'll allow, give her as many pets and treats as she wants. Despite clearing out your apartment, you've spoiled her. She licks the scales on your cheek as you cry over her. This seems to inspire something in her; she demands her tuna crunchies. Dutifully you give her the treats. She can have as many tuna crunchies as she wants.

Doomscrolling your twitter feed, you make sure this isn't the day you lose access to your meds because of some white man in a suit. A sister is assaulted by a violent extremist with a sense of humor: he shot her with a harpoon gun. Her crowdfunding campaign starts on the maidens subreddit and goes viral.

You triple check to make sure your friend is still willing to take the cat when you go. They promise to spoil her and tell her stories of you every day. You continue to cry over it. They invite you out for sushi to talk about it, then backtrack and ask if that's a microaggression. You go to sushi. You're thankful for the distraction.

By the time your legs are more scale than skin and your fingers begin to develop webbing, you've given up on pretense. The looks are now constant, but you get reflective sunglasses and a new patch for your jacket: *Don't like it? Drown,* with a scaled hand reaching out of water and flipping the bird. You put that energy out into the world, and the world doesn't fuck with you.

Children love you. Their parents do not.

On the train, a young girl quietly asks if she can feel your scales. You allow her to touch her little fingers to the aquamarine pattern running up your arm, giving her your most reassuring (but still fanged) smile. She's fearless, enamored, reverent. The mother pulls her daughter away and hastily apologizes for her, not looking you in the eye. But you know that girl believes in magic now.

A group of white supremacists go out on a boat loaded with assault rifles for "no reason" and get lost at sea. This is somehow your fault.

The day your fins begin to push their way out from your arms, your boss calls you into his office. You both know he can't fire you in this and seven other states, but you both also know you won't be staying much longer. He's done his best to make you aware you're making his life more difficult. You put in your two weeks before he can flounder for another excuse. He maroons you with paperwork for the rest of the afternoon.

Someone leaves a rotting fish in your pool locker. You don't go back and don't file a report. You tell yourself the chlorine was bad for the gills freshly forming under your ribs anyway.

Your friends take you out clubbing. You lose yourself under the waves of music, submerged under strobe lights and the salty sweat of dancing bodies. You whisper sweet nothings into a stranger's ear, entrancing her as you move against each other. You can see iridescence shining around her eyes, shimmering glitter and an emerging pattern beneath makeup. You brush a thumb against her cheek and she melts into your touch. You don't get her name. You don't need to; you're both not long for this world. You catch up with your friends smoking outside, lips still tingling with vermouth.

Weeks pass. Work ends. Your apartment is down to furniture and cat supplies. You take longer showers. News stories continue to come out, the machine churns and roils: monsters walking among humans, the mark of the beast, sacrificing daughters to the ocean.

You make sure your meds are re-upped for the final stretch.

When your legs start to merge you know you don't have much time left. You donate the last boxes of your clothes. Your friends get first dibs on furniture before it's put on the street. They bring drinks and sit on your floor, an impromptu celebration and wake. They ask all the usual questions: What are you going to do for food? Shelter? What if you get hurt, or attacked by a shark? Do they have waterproof laptops yet? Will they ever see you again? What if it isn't right for you? Can you ever come back?

You don't know how to answer most of those questions. The group stays up, drinking through the night. At 4AM you put on The Little Mermaid and the group drunkenly sings along. Everyone knows the words. It's juvenile and you can hear the maidens on the subreddit rolling their eyes and tutting about misrepresentation, but you know everyone in your position does it. You try not to cry, but the waterworks start and don't stop.

At daybreak you put your cat into her harness and everyone piles into a friend's van. It's not far to the beach, but they take the long way around. One final tour of the land. Your cat sits on your lap and stares out the windows as you pass old haunts: your grocery store, your gym, your high school. You realize you still have library books to return and almost get them to turn around, but someone promises to go back for them afterwards.

There's an isolated area on the beach where a canopy and tables are set up; banners, food, friends. It's a regular going away party, as if you're going on a short trip abroad. You suppose you are, in a way. Someone rented a wheelchair with fat tires to help you get down to the beach.

When your mother arrives, she pulls her shirt off to show her custom-made clam bra. Her eyes are already red and puffy, but she's doing her best to be energetic and upbeat. She holds you for a long time and says she's happy for you, that you're beautiful, that you're so much stronger than she ever was, and then she puts on a brave face to help everyone get served at the buffet. Your cat chases small crabs across the beach around you, and you sit in the sand. The party goes strong.

The tides come up until your fin is tickled by the seafoam. Everyone knows that means it's time to go. You pass your cat off to her new owner and she gives you one last headbutt. She seems to understand. You kiss your mother's cheek one last time and she clings to you. The group raises their drinks as you paddle out, disappearing beneath the waves. You give them the money shot and leap out of the water on your way out of the sound. You can hear cheering from the shoreline. You hope someone got a video for the maidens.

You keep the city in sight for a while, but the current leads you further into open waters. There are boaters out on the water who wave to you. You wave back and keep swimming up the coast.

At dusk you rise to the surface and watch the setting sun turn the horizon from blue to pink to purple and orange. There's nothing for leagues around. As the sun sinks below the waves and the skies darken, you sing your first real siren's song. Shaky and imperfect, it soon resounds over the ocean breeze. You leave everything behind in it. There are no words, only feeling and sound. It's a lament, an invocation, a dirge. It is many things, but it isn't an apology. You have nothing to apologize for.

In the seas beyond, a chorus joins in with a language you never learned but understand, integrating your song into theirs. You swim to join them.

ABOUT EMMERYN PALLADINO

Emmeryn Palladino is an author and game designer with degrees from NYU and Manhattanville college. When she isn't designing worlds she's working on her debut novel and thinking about being a big lesbian, sometimes at the same time. Follow her writing Twitter at @Emmerynwrites or her personal twitter @gamemakerm

AFTER THE WAR

VALERIE HUNTER

When he left the King's service after the war, Lias was given the same option as every soldier: a small pouch of coins or the opportunity to relocate to the newly-acquired territory jokingly referred to as the end of the earth. Those who accepted the second offer received a parcel of land with a house, two dray horses, a wagon and plow, enough sorghum seed to cultivate the entire acreage, three hens and a rooster, and other necessary supplies. It was a much better deal, so Lias took it. He could be a one-armed farmer as easily as a one-armed anything else.

He headed to the end of the earth by wagon train, and, once there, a land warden assigned him a farm. Lias volunteered for a plot far from the closest villages and roads. He tried not to think about who might have lived in the small house last, whether they had been displaced or executed or killed in battle. Some things were best not dwelt on.

Among the supplies he'd been given was a fat handbook on farming and survival, which he read multiple times that first spring. Its tone was straightforward and unsympathetic, and it was written for people with two arms and a background in agri-culture, but Lias still found it useful. With the help of the book and his horses, he plowed the land and planted the sorghum. With the help of the book and a lot of patience, he scavenged the countryside for edible plants to add to his food supply. With the help of the book and his own ingenuity with a scythe, he harvested the sorghum one-handed and got it to the mill, which earned him enough money to survive the winter and begin the process again come spring.

In between the work and the reading and the planning, Lias drew. He'd taught himself to do many things with his left hand after the loss of his right — all the necessities of working and cooking and living — but drawing was hardest. Maybe because it had been the one thing that had come most naturally before. Maybe because it was something he wanted so badly to do well — no shortcuts, no cheating, no accepting good enough.

Regardless, the pencil felt alien in his fingers. He'd already mastered left-handed writing, but this was different. He spent two months just drawing lines, trying to get his hand to do what he wanted. He didn't have much paper, so he used the margins of the handbook or just drew in the air, extending the pencil and his arm and trying to ignore how wrong it felt to do this so purposelessly.

Eventually he graduated to sketching leaves, clouds, anything with a definitive shape that he could wrap his mind around. Frequently the shapes he saw looked nothing like the shapes that ended up on his paper, but he persisted. He couldn't stop.

His old sketchbook sat on the shelf, containing every sketch he'd ever made back when he had two hands. The paper was pulpy and coarse. He'd bound it himself using a piece of thick sailcloth for the cover. It was the only thing he'd brought with him from the orphanage, and it was what had gotten him out of the orphanage in the first place. "We can always use talent like yours," the recruiter said, and Lias had been eager to go.

He could remember that. He could remember the years of war, what he learned to do, the role he played. He could remember drawing in his book whenever he had the energy.

But he couldn't remember the end and what had happened to his arm.

That worried him. If he could forget something so momentous, what else might be missing? And what did it say about the state of his mind, that things could get lost up there?

His sketchbook held the answers. He knew that, and still he didn't open it. He told himself it would be cheating; he wanted to remember on his own, without any assistance.

Really, though, he didn't want to look at his old drawings until his new ones were better. He knew his current skills were subpar, and a direct comparison would only rub salt in the wound. He'd wait until he improved, and in the meantime perhaps he'd remember on his own.

Winter gave him plenty of time to sketch, and when spring came again he fell back into the routine of hard work, plowing, and planting. It was easy enough to believe he really was at the end of the earth. His neighbors all lived well away; the adjoining farm was untenanted.

And then it wasn't. One morning he went outside and saw a wagon next door full of something he couldn't identify.

He walked over with trepidation. He hadn't talked to anyone but his horses in months. Suppose his ability to be friendly had fallen into the same hole as the memory of his arm?

He passed a field of sorghum he'd just planted but was actually on the neighbor's land. When no one had moved in by planting time, he figured the land would lie fallow, so why shouldn't he utilize it? A stupid decision, clearly.

A dog came racing at him as he got closer, small and mottled with a surprisingly deep bark. It ran circles around Lias, barely managing not to trip him. A larger, calmer dog emerged from the barn along with the neighbor, a young woman with cropped hair and trousers. He pegged her for a soldier rather than a soldier's wife.

She nodded to him. "You live on the next farm?"

He nodded back. "Lias Wynton."

"I'm Senna. This is Tal," — she put a hand on the big dog's head — "and the little nuisance is Nim." With a final bark, the smaller dog flopped at her mistress's feet.

"You need help unloading?" He could now see the wagon was full of plants, their roots carefully bundled.

She stared at his pinned-up sleeve. "Nah, I'm fine."

He knew a dismissal when he heard one, but he still couldn't help asking. "What are they?"

"Fruit trees."

He looked again. Of course he knew that trees had to start somewhere, but these looked so puny that he couldn't imagine them ever getting large. "This is what they allotted you?" It hardly seemed fair.

"No, I got sorghum, same as everyone. But I don't want to be a sorghum farmer."

"Then how are you going to live?" he asked. He might not know much about fruit trees, but he knew those puny plants wouldn't produce anything edible for years, if they survived at all.

"I sold most of the sorghum seed and the second horse for a start; that'll see me through for a while."

He stared at her as though she'd said something remarkable. They'd all been given seed, and judging by how busy the mill had been last fall, no one had thought to do anything other than plant them. They'd never been told they had to. Of course it only took some imagination to do otherwise.

"Anyhow, this field is yours," he mumbled, pointing. "I had extra seed. Didn't know you'd be coming. You can have the proceeds."

"That's hardly fair when you planted it, and you'll be the one harvesting it."

"It's your land."

She frowned. "Give me a small percentage, then. Is it too late to plant more? I've got two sacks of seed I didn't sell, if you want to plant those, too."

He agreed and left, his head awhirl. She seemed even less

inclined to friendliness than he did, her tone harsh, her blazing eyes all but slicing into him, and yet she hadn't been unkind.

He tried to draw her that night, but he couldn't capture a single one of her features. He'd have to get used to her before he could do it right.

Over the next few days he planted her sorghum while she planted the trees. They looked even more stunted in the ground, like spindly babies that needed protection. He wanted to warn her they'd never survive, but her expression, even from a distance, was so fierce that he held his tongue.

He went back to his own fields after that, but he could see her each day going to and fro from her well to water the trees. Would she be able to keep that up day after day? Of course it was none of his business.

But one day, a few weeks later, he noticed an easel in the yard, and he couldn't help walking closer. Senna painted quickly and confidently, the colors blooming from her brush. The familiar movement of it made his chest ache.

"You're a mage," he blurted out.

Senna startled and dropped the brush. Nim, who had been napping under the easel, gave a sharp bark, and Tal cocked his head. Senna turned to him, frowning. "No."

Lias wasn't sure he believed her. He'd known mages who weren't artists, but no artists who weren't mages. "Sorry. I didn't mean to startle you. You're very talented."

She shrugged and retrieved the brush, went back to adding colors that shouldn't belong but did. "Why'd you think I was a mage?"

"A lot of artists are," he said. "Casting a spell is akin to drawing or painting. The motion."

"Well, aren't you knowledgeable." She looked at him with narrowed eyes, and he thought he'd said too much, but she turned back, dappling specks of yellow light across the prairie. She removed the paper and tacked on a fresh one. "Want to try?"

His fingers itched to take the brush, but he shook his head. "No. I'd best be getting back."

He hurried away, not caring if he was being rude. He'd stick to his pencil, to black and gray absolutes. Color was too easy to drown in.

That evening he drew Senna's hand over and over, the paintbrush an extension of her fingers. He wondered if she'd held a sword the same way during the war, if she'd had magic pulsing through that as well. Surely someone would have noticed, but then again people could be exceedingly blind.

Senna sought him out a few days later. "I need a hand."

"Well, I do have one."

She snorted. "The door of the house was a bit warped. I took it off and planed it, but I could use help getting it back on."

He followed her to the house where she held the door in place while he reinserted the hinges.

Neither of them spoke until Senna said, "You're just as bad at this as I am."

"What?" he asked, confused. The door was nearly finished.

"Small talk."

That was true enough. "I haven't had much chance to practice."

"Lucky you. I've got the Mallotts on my other side, with their eighty-seven small, curious children."

Lias laughed. He'd helped Mr. Mallott deepen his well last summer and had given up trying to count the exact number of Mallott offspring, though he thought they numbered under a dozen. They all moved quickly, but one little boy had sidled over long enough to ask Lias what had happened to his arm.

"A dragon ate it," he said, and the boy gaped at him before scuttling away. Lias was sorry afterwards — suppose he gave the poor kid nightmares? — but it was the first thing that had popped into his head. And surely any answer was better than saying he didn't remember.

"Anyhow, you're preferable to them," Senna said.

"Well, we're both trying, aren't we?" he said. When she just looked at him, he added, "At being neighborly. I think we're doing all right for two people without much experience."

She smiled, which made her eyes dance. He spent the whole evening trying to capture that smile on paper. He didn't quite succeed, but he thought he'd get there, eventually.

The next time he noticed her painting, he walked over again. Nim barked, and Senna said hello without turning around.

A garden had sprung up in front of her house. He'd seen her plant it weeks ago, but he'd thought it was vegetables, like his own. It was flowers. They seemed to have blossomed all at once in a tangled patch of color. He drank them in with his eyes, tried to store up their soft, curling shapes so he could draw them later.

"It's beautiful," he said.

"My painting or the garden?"

She was painting the flowers; the colors were different but the riotous beauty was the same. "Both."

"Huh. I thought you'd say the garden was impractical. I did plant vegetables, too, behind the house."

"I think the flowers are just as important."

"They won't fill any bellies."

No, but they filled something else, something just as vital. He tried to find the words to say that, but he couldn't. He looked up to see two of the middle-sized Mallott children approaching on a sorry-looking mule. The boy mumbled an invitation to a summer solstice party in three days' time.

"A party?" Senna asked, like the word was foreign.

Both children nodded.

"We'll come," Lias said.

Senna shot him a glare but didn't contradict him. "A party," she repeated scornfully once the mule was out of sight.

"We're practicing our neighborliness," he reminded her, and she laughed.

Last summer Lias had found a glut of blackberries and taught himself, through trial and error, how to make a pie that wasn't tough as rawhide or soggy straight through. The berries weren't abundant yet this year, but he gleaned all he could, enough for two pies which would hopefully be enough for eighty-seven children and several adults.

On the afternoon of the party, he scrubbed himself, put on a clean shirt, and headed over to Senna's with his basket of pies. She was similarly scrubbed, and had a large bouquet.

The dogs accompanied them, Tal in step with Senna, Nim repeatedly dashing ahead and circling back. When they reached the Mallotts', the yard awash in shrieking children, Nim immediately joined in their game while Tal slunk to the shade of the barn. Mrs. Mallott greeted them heartily and arranged Senna's flowers at the center of the long table.

They sat down to eat, the food delicious and plentiful, and it gave Lias the chance to count the Mallott offspring.

"Nine," he whispered to Senna under the cover of clinking cutlery.

"And a half," she muttered back, and he blushed because he shouldn't be noticing Mrs. Mallott's condition.

During the pie, the little boy who'd asked about his arm said, "Pa told me dragons don't exist. What really happened to you?"

The rest of the Mallotts were carrying on their own conversations, but Lias saw Senna pause, clearly listening.

"A swyrth," he said quickly, naming the ferocious, bear-like creatures that roamed the outskirts of the kingdom. "Chomped it right off."

The boy stared at him, and Lias stared back until the boy returned to his pie.

Once they'd finished eating, Mr. Mallott took out his fiddle and the air filled with music. The Mallott children danced across the yard like sprites, and to Lias's surprise Senna got up and swung the smaller children. They screamed with delight.

The littlest girl held out her hand to Lias, and he twirled her as she giggled. Fireflies dotted the growing twilight, and he planned how he'd draw everything later, all those spinning, joyous children.

The fiddle zipped into a different song, Mr. Mallott's voice melancholy as he sang.

> *"When the war is over, my love*
> *and the magic's been put away,*
> *I'll tell you a tale of the brave and the true*
> *if you'll remember those long ago days."*

The little girl spun herself dizzy and flopped onto the grass. Lias backed away, the song crawling against his skin. It was from a war long before this last one. He'd heard it a hundred times before. So why did it squeeze at him now, bringing a dark cloud that hazed over his mind and made his heart pound?

Senna came over. "You've gone strange."

"I'm fine," he mumbled.

She grabbed his hand and pulled him along until he was spinning with her. The motion distorted the music, and by the time the song ended he was thoroughly dizzy but otherwise fine.

They left shortly after, before the sun had completely gone. The music followed them a long while, otherworldly in the near-dark but no longer frightening. It was a lovely night, and they didn't ruin it by speaking.

When he got home, he skipped drawing, afraid if he tried to capture the beauty of the party, the black cloud of that song might infringe and ruin it. He'd try tomorrow, when the song was no longer looping its way through his head, surrounding the hole in his memory like a spiked fence.

Lias didn't see much of Senna for weeks after the party, but he did notice her ride out one afternoon in the direction of the Mallotts' wearing a sword, which made him stare. She didn't come back all day, but the next morning she was watering her trees, same as always.

It was perhaps five days later when Nim came, barking insistently at Lias's door and then weaving her way around his feet like he was a sheep she meant to herd. "All right, I'm coming," he muttered, trying to pretend he wasn't alarmed.

He set a good pace to Senna's, but Nim wasn't satisfied, hurrying him along. The door to the house was ajar. Lias hesitated, but Nim barreled ahead so he followed.

Senna was on the bed, tangled in the blanket, face flushed deep red, muttering and shouting by turn. Tal sat like a sentinel and gave Lias a pleading look.

He knew little about illness, but he'd have to make do. He fetched fresh water, then untangled Senna from the blanket. A terrible heat radiated off her. He propped her up, sponged her face, and held a cup to her lips. "Drink."

She swallowed a few sips before snarling something about a swyrth.

"Mm-hmm," he agreed. "Another sip, go on."

She sipped, then seemed to register his presence. "Lias? I'm hot."

"You're ill."

She groaned. "Stupid Mallotts. Eighty-seven children down with the red ague." She flopped back against him. "Powders. Under the bed."

He thought she was raving again, but she repeated it until he looked. Sure enough a small crate under the bed held various bottles and packets that looked medicinal in nature, though none were labeled. He jostled Senna's arm. "Which one?"

Her eyes fluttered, but she gestured to the largest packet. "A pinch of that in boiling water for fever."

He prepared it, made her drink it. Fifteen minutes later she was sleeping peacefully, her face less flushed.

He left her there with the dogs for nurses and got on with his day. There was hay to cut, a hot and tiring job, but he went back to check on her at noon and again that evening, mixing up more fever drink, caring for her animals, watering her trees.

The next morning she seemed a little better, but she was still fretful and pink-cheeked. He made her tea and porridge, and sat with her while she ate, taking a good look around the room for the first time. A sword hung over the mantle, shiny and ornate with the King's own insignia worked into the hilt. Not the sword of a yeoman soldier. "You were King's Guard?" he said, surprised.

She grunted. He didn't say anything more, but he wondered. King's Guard was a lifetime appointment, not something that ended with the war. What was Senna doing here?

She improved a little each day, to the point where she could coherently curse the Mallott children for spreading pestilence. He was tempted to ask what she'd been doing there, why she'd brought her sword, but he sensed this would upset her, and it was no good upsetting people when they'd been ill.

"You'll be sick with it next," she warned. "Better take some fever powder with you."

He could already feel a tell-tale throbbing behind his eyes, but he was doing his best to ignore it. "I'll be fine."

He kept telling himself that, even when he woke the next morning feeling impossibly hot. After drinking three cups of water, he decided he felt better and could finish the haying.

The sun seemed excessively bright and pulsing. Maybe someone had cast a spell on it. Were there sun spells? Surely not, but he couldn't remember. He should summon some clouds. He raised his arm, then stared at the absence. He swore he could feel it burning —

No. That was foolishness. He swung the scythe, putting his

whole body into it to make up for the part that wasn't there. Again and again. He swung too hard and his lungs ejected from his chest. He sank to his knees, searching for them.

The next thing he knew there was a damp pressure against his cheek. Nim. He pushed her away, but with the hand he didn't have, so nothing happened.

"Lias! Oh, for pity's sake!"

Senna. She wet his face, and he could swear his skin sizzled. She held the canteen to his mouth, and he swallowed "Can you get up or shall I fetch the horse?" She sounded angry.

He tried to rise, and Senna hauled him up by his good arm and dragged him along, cursing. "At least I had the good sense to stay in bed! What were you thinking? You're lucky you didn't collapse on the scythe."

He didn't remember much after that, just how lovely and cool his bed felt. When he woke up next, it no longer felt cool and Senna was forcing some terrible concoction down his throat. She was still there the next time he woke, and the next.

Finally he woke to find her gone, but Nim sat by the bed. The little dog lacked Tal's gravitas, but she gave Lias a hopeful smile that was rather comforting.

Senna came the next morning, forcing a foul-tasting broth on him. "Thought you were a goner for awhile there," she said frowning, and he bit back the urge to apologize because he knew she wouldn't take it well. You got to know a person once you'd been ill together.

He choked down the broth silently, but as she was leaving he said, "Thank you."

She scowled. "Don't thank me. I'm the one who got you sick." She slammed out of the house, but she left Nim. He noticed her painting of the garden tacked to the wall opposite his bed, all those beautiful, chaotic colors.

She checked on him a few more times after that, but he told her he just needed rest and she let him be. He propped himself up in bed and drew — the folds of his blanket, Nim's eager eyes, the black hole in his dreams that he'd nearly fallen into. Senna's hovering face with its mixture of anger and concern that he could nearly capture.

When he finally left the house, the sun no longer seemed menacing. He probably wasn't up to cutting the rest of the hay yet, but he should at least rescue his scythe.

But when he got there, the scythe was gone and so was the hay. He went back to the barn and found the scythe hanging on the wall, the hay drying in the loft.

He walked over to Senna's, ostensibly to return Nim. He knew how she felt about thank yous. He found her watering the orchard.

"They look bigger," he offered. The trees were toddler-sized now instead of babies.

She shrugged.

"Did the hay give you any trouble?"

"Nah. I got the oldest Mallott boy to help me. I don't know how you manage that scythe one-handed, though."

"Necessity." He paused. "You're welcome, by the way."

"What for?"

He grinned. "Giving you the opportunity to practice being neighborly."

Her laughter filled the orchard.

Lias felt stronger each day after that. He didn't see much of Senna, but Nim visited frequently, romping over to check that Lias was still upright and breathing.

Sometimes Senna rode out with her sword, disappeared for half the day, and both dogs wandered over to Lias's. Of course they couldn't tell him what she was up to, and he didn't dare ask her. He knew it was none of his business.

But curiosity finally got the better of him, and he decided to wait up for her. She always returned late, so this time he stayed outside, even went over and watered the trees for her. It hadn't rained in ages.

The dogs heard the horse before he did and raced toward it.

Lias followed slowly, not wanting to show his eagerness, his relief. He got close enough to see that Senna was leading the horse. Had it thrown a shoe? No, there was something draped over the saddle, a large mass —

He stopped dead, catching the gamy scent as his eyes made sense of what he was seeing. A swyrth. She'd killed a swyrth.

He picked up his pace. "Are you all right?"

She scowled. "I'm fine."

She had a crude bandage wrapped around her forearm, and even in the waning light he could see blood seeping through it. "Let me tend your arm."

"Stop fussing, Lias." The words snapped from her tongue.

She led the horse into the barn and he followed, watching as she yanked the swyrth to the floor with a thump. He had so many questions, but he knew she wouldn't answer.

Then he noticed the pile in the far stall. A stack of furs, at least half a dozen.

"You go hunting them," he said, looking from the stack to Senna.

She shot him a look like he was an idiot for just realizing this now.

He was tired of her looks, tired of watching what he said. "Of all the stupid . . . why would you go hunting swyrths?"

Her glare intensified. "They're there. They need killing. I'm good at it, and the furs are valuable."

"It's dangerous!" Swyrth hunting in the kingdom entailed a group with powerful bows, not a single person with a sword.

"What would you know about it? I'm more of a soldier than you ever were, not some little girl who needs protecting."

"I know that, but —"

"You don't know anything. You're just a coward who sees danger in every shadow." She sneered, disgust dripping from every word. "You should be glad I killed the swyrth before it could come and eat your other arm, eh?"

He walked out of the barn. Nim followed halfheartedly, but Lias shooed her back and she went.

He was still seething once he got home, but he sat down to draw anyway. He captured Senna's snarl, the rage sparking in her eyes. The sadness, too. He hadn't seen it at the time but it was there now, staring up from the page. He wasn't sure if he was drawing true or if he'd added it in because he wanted it to be there, wanted her to be as damaged and wounded as him instead of cruel and awful.

He turned the page so he didn't have to look at her anymore and sketched a swyrth. He'd never seen a live one, but he used his imagination, turned it into a nightmarish beast with enormous claws and pointy teeth, but also Senna's sad eyes.

He put the book back on the shelf beside the sketchbook. He stared at them both for a long time, his past and his present, then touched the sketchbook's spine. Maybe now was the time. Maybe if he opened it, remembered everything, he would know what to say to Senna, know how not to run from her anger and her sadness.

He went to bed. He was a coward through and through, too scared to open the book, not because of what might be in there, but because it might not work. If he looked through it and still couldn't remember, he was afraid something inside of him might break in a way that could never be fixed.

Lias and Senna ignored one another after that. It wasn't easy, but it was for the best. He didn't need to spend his days worrying about her.

Of course worrying didn't work that way. He continued to sneak glances in the direction of her farm, but he never saw her go off with her sword. When he glimpsed her she was tending the orchard or the gardens, the dogs shadowing her every step.

He didn't want to draw her anymore so he drew the fruit trees instead, trying to capture their tenuous strength. They seemed bigger each day, infused with a magic he was convinced Senna had, even if she wouldn't acknowledge it.

Summer waned, hot and dry. It would be autumn soon, and he'd have to venture on to Senna's land to harvest the extra sorghum. He would have to talk to her, too, when he brought her the money from the milling, unless he just left it on her doorstep in the dead of night.

He was on the barn roof fixing some loose shingles when he saw a swarm of jackrabbits race past. He turned, and it took him a moment to comprehend what he was seeing. A dark cloud rose like magic, and he found himself leaning towards it, reaching with the arm he didn't have to contribute to whatever was brewing.

Then the wind shifted and he could smell it. Not magic. Fire.

He scrambled down the ladder to see Senna running toward him, the dogs flanking her.

"What do we do?" Senna asked. Her voice sounded hollow, like she wasn't really expecting an answer. More jackrabbits ran past, and Lias longed to follow them, away from that menacing wall of flames.

There was a chapter on wildfire in the farming handbook. It advised taking a ladder and climbing into the depths of your well. It didn't mention what to do if, like Mallott, you had a pregnant wife and eighty-seven children who might not all fit. It didn't mention what to do afterwards, when you climbed back up and found your world obliterated.

"We stop it," he told Senna, looking at the sky above the smoke. "We conjure a storm."

"I'm not a mage!"

He knew she was. No one could paint like her, grow an orchard and a garden like hers, without at least a pinch of magic coursing through their blood. But convincing her would take time they didn't have, so he just said, "I am."

She looked at him. No, she was looking at his absence of an arm. "You can't —"

"*We* can," he insisted. "You'll do the casting. I'll show you how. You'll draw on my magic. Do you trust me?"

The skepticism didn't leave her face, but she nodded. That was all he needed. Her trust.

"Get your paintbrush," he said. She didn't question this bizarre request, just went, the dogs at her heels.

He'd never created a rainstorm before. He'd called up a dust storm to overwhelm a surprise advance, and a hailstorm once as well, early in the war. Power sharing among mages had involved a metal snake that they'd each held onto with their non-dominant hand, binding them in a circle. He remembered the horrible tingling sensation of it as he both fed and drew magic.

By the last year of the war it wasn't storms anymore, it was people. A circle of ten mages, pooling their power and concentration, could squeeze the air from someone's lungs, the blood from someone's heart. It took tremendous effort, but it was effective. Their targets were chosen for them carefully — the smartest and bravest of enemy commanders, the most powerful noblemen.

Lias's stomach contracted. He'd always puked after such spells, as though he could empty the wrongness from his body. He reminded himself that he wouldn't be using his magic for destruction today.

The fire grew closer, an advancing army assured of victory. He felt an overwhelming desire to scuttle down the well, but he reminded himself he was a mage and had faced worse than this.

Senna returned with the paintbrush. "Can't you do it?" she asked. "Left-handed?"

He didn't remind her that she'd been convinced he couldn't just minutes before, didn't tell her he was tempted to try. "I'd be too slow. I need you."

He positioned himself behind her so he could hold her left hand in his own, locking their fingers together in a tight knot. A power share between two people was both much simpler and much more dangerous than a circle. The person casting the spell could drain too much energy, kill their partner, but he couldn't tell Senna that or she might not want to try.

"Can you feel it?" he asked. She nodded, her curls tickling his cheek. It wasn't the sickening tingle he'd gotten on the battlefield, just a pulse of pure energy that made him feel they could do anything.

"I'm going to say the spell while you cast it," he said. "Think about rain, and then, with the brush, paint a storm in the air."

He let his words sink in for a moment. The air crackled. Nim whined, long and pitiful.

"That's all?" Senna asked.

He remembered how ridiculous he'd felt the first time he'd cast, following his master's instructions with a pencil in his hand. It had worked, though, and eventually the pencil hadn't been necessary.

"That's all. But you have to do it with confidence. All your concentration and energy need to be on that storm. Ready?"

She nodded, squeezed his hand even tighter.

"Go!"

Her arm shot up, the paintbrush a blur of motion. Lias leaned into her, chanting the spell in rhythm with her movements. They were one body, one purpose, their hands melded together, their magic —

Crack!

He fell, backward and backward and back. The war was over and he was celebrating, a banquet hall full of mages all abuzz with their victory. But they sobered quickly when the Grand Mage rose and began to speak.

"You have accomplished great things under my command, sons and daughters. The war would not be over without the combined force of your powers. Now the kingdom must ask one more sacrifice of you."

The hall was full, but the Grand Mage looked at each of them individually, taking her time as her gaze traveled the room.

"The kingdom needed you desperately, and you answered that

call. However, such power comes at a price. To do what you have done, so well and for so long, takes its toll. Now that the war is over, the magic inside you is too much for everyday life. It will fester, corrupt, compel you to cause unbelievable destruction before it kills you altogether.

"You have a choice. You can give your life for all that is pure and good in the kingdom, die like the heroes you are and be remembered for everything you've done, including this final sacrifice. Or you can give up your casting arm and live a magic-less life, the power drained through the loss of your limb. The choice is yours. Think it over, and enjoy your meal."

The Grand Mage withdrew to stunned silence. And then they began to murmur, to talk, to mourn already for the lives they were about to lose. They were heroes, all of them. They were not giving up their arms.

"Lias!"

The voice was far away. He was at the banquet, amongst his mates. Some of them began to sing.

When the war is over, my love . . .

"Lias, wake up!"

Senna sounded terrified. He wanted to get to her, but his body was limp, and he couldn't feel his arm — his left arm. His only arm —

Panic squeezed his lungs shut, turned him cold. He couldn't —

And the magic's been put away . . .

"Lias!"

He forced his eyes open. His face was wet. His tears, or Senna's? No, it was raining, a hard, soaking rain. He drew a breath, shook his arm out. It was still numb, but it tingled a little. He told himself it would be all right, it would all be all right because the fire was dying under the assault of raindrops and the thunder was roaring a victory cry.

Senna pulled him up by the armpits. "I thought I'd killed

you!" she said. She sounded angry but he could hear the terror beneath the rage.

"You didn't!" he yelled above the storm "You did this!"

"*We* did this," she corrected. "Now can we get inside before we drown?"

They stumbled into his house. The dogs shook themselves and lay down, and Lias took out dry clothes for himself and Senna, then turned toward the wall to dress. He felt like he was still in some far recess of his mind, the memories hitting him in waves. He got himself mostly dressed, but his left hand remained tingly and strange and he couldn't manage the buttons.

Senna came over and nudged his fumbling hand away, did up his shirt quickly even though he could see her own hands trembling. She led him over to a chair, pushed him into it, then put the kettle on to boil. "A hot drink will do us both good," she said, as though tea might keep him from falling apart. "The rain will stop eventually, won't it? We're not going to have to build an ark?"

"It'll stop," he said, his voice raw.

When she put the mugs down and sat across from him, she said, "I loved to draw when I was a little girl. My grandmother made me stop. She was a mage; she knew the signs. She knew that war was coming, too, and that mages didn't fare well after wars. She knew a lot, my grandmother."

He stared at her. She'd known, all this time.

"I took up a sword instead," she went on. "When I was accepted into the King's Guard at sixteen, I was overjoyed. I knew what I'd be doing the rest of my life." She stared into her tea as though seeing this old life.

"What changed?" he asked when she didn't go on.

She gave him that scathing look meant to eviscerate him. "I killed people."

He held her gaze. "So did I."

She shook her head. "It's not the same."

"They're still dead."

"But you paid for it."

It took him a moment to catch her meaning. "My arm? You think that's . . . penance?"

She shrugged. "Isn't it?"

"Shall I chop off your arm so you can't wield a sword, see if that makes you feel less guilty?" When she didn't answer, he said, "It was war, Senna. You did what you had to do."

"You don't know what I did!"

"So tell me."

Her eyes were afire with rage and defiance, and, underneath, so much sadness. "After the war," she said, barely above a whisper. "All those mages."

His ghost arm throbbed. "You did the amputations?"

"No. I did the beheadings."

He found it suddenly difficult to breathe, saw the faces of his mates that last night. They'd all said death was preferable to losing their magic, but he'd said that, too, and here he sat.

"How many?" he choked out.

"I lost count."

"Was . . . was it only you? Executing them?"

She shook her head. "Half a dozen of us. We killed over a hundred mages."

The entire mage battalion had numbered 150. How many lived? Forty? Ten?

Just him?

"I felt sick the entire time," Senna said. "I wanted to say something, wanted to refuse, but all I could hear was my grandmother telling me it wasn't safe to be a mage."

"You followed orders. What else could you have done? They were the ones who had a choice." Even as he said it he felt disloyal. It had been a choice so terrible that his own memory had refused to hold onto it.

"How did you end up here?" he asked.

"I waited a year, so as not to raise suspicion, and then I ate myssip root. Causes heart palpitations while it's in your system. I was declared unfit for service, and I asked to retire out here. I wanted to start over, lead a better life. Be a completely different person. Someone I could live with. But every night when I go to bed, all I see are the mages I killed."

"So you hunt swyrths hoping they might kill you?"

She shook her head. "To try to atone. And because I enjoy fighting, which is a terrible thing to enjoy, but it's acceptable when you're killing swyrths. There was a whole colony of them out past the Mallotts' place. I didn't want any of those eighty-seven children getting eaten."

"And if you got eaten instead?"

"Well, it would serve me right, wouldn't it?"

"No, it wouldn't," he said firmly, but he knew she needed to hear more than that. "If you want to talk about atonement, you just saved the livelihoods of half the countryside."

She waved her hand, like it was nothing.

"Besides," he said, "the world doesn't work on *deserve*. Those mages didn't deserve to die. You didn't deserve to be forced to kill them. None of us deserved to have to fight in a war when we were little more than children being told what to do."

The rain was quieter now against the roof, though still steady. Nim came and lay on his feet as though realizing Lias needed something to anchor him.

He bent to stroke the dog's ears, keeping his gaze on Senna. "Do you know, for the longest time I couldn't remember how I lost my arm. Couldn't remember the choice I made."

"Lucky you," she said.

"No, it was terrible. An enormous hole that I was always hovering on the edge of, afraid I'd fall in."

"But you remember now?"

He nodded. The memory felt new and fresh, like it had been polished to a shine in all that time he'd been forgetting it. He told her what the Grand Mage had said, and how the banquet afterwards had lasted all night. "We were the heroes of the kingdom, and tomorrow we would die, but that night we meant to live.

"The longer it went on, though, the more songs that were

sung and adventures recounted, the more I didn't want to be there. So I went back to my room." He got up, took the sketchbook from the shelf. "I was always drawing; I figured I might as well spend my last night doing the thing I loved most. So I did. I drew my mates. I drew the magic we cast, the chaos we created. I drew myself." This last sketch was hazy in his mind; he'd been so tired when he'd gotten to it. "And all that time I didn't think anything other than I was going to give my life because I wouldn't want to live without this. Not the magic. The drawing.

"And then morning came, and the guard asked, 'Your arm or your head?' Not, 'Your magic or your life?' Just, 'Your arm or your head?' And I thought, *Well, I have another arm. No coming back from the head*, so I said, 'Arm.' Simple as that.

"And afterwards, when I didn't remember choosing at all, I still remembered that I was a mage and I was an artist. And it didn't matter much about the magic, but I meant to draw again."

He curled his fingers more tightly around the sketchbook. All this time he'd been too scared to open it, afraid of what abyss he might tumble into if he did. Now he knew, yet he still felt the same ache to open it, the same apprehension. He could see all he'd lost, see how far or close he was to being what he once was. See that last sketch, look his old self in the eyes.

He went to the stove and pushed the sketchbook in, watching as the pages caught and curled, crumbled away. "That book haunted me all this time," he said into the flames. "I don't need the past to tell me who I am now."

He turned back to Senna, who was watching the stove like she expected a ghost to emerge. "I would've liked to have seen your drawings," she said.

He fetched the farming handbook and handed it to her. "Here."

She opened it, flipped through all his early efforts, the lines that refused to obey, the wonky shapes and perspectives. She got to a page of the dogs and smiled, tracing the lines with the tip of her finger. He looked away, unable to watch anymore.

"You draw me a lot," she said. He couldn't quite read her tone, but it wasn't scathing. She was looking at the page where he'd drawn her when she was painting. "You capture so much, so simply. You knew I was a mage, even then."

He nodded. "You knew I was one, too."

"I suspected." She paused "Do you believe that Grand Mage? That you were corrupted? That you had to give up your life or your magic?"

"I don't know."

"Maybe it's just something they said, because a kingdom full of powerful, trained wizards might overthrow the king."

"Maybe."

She scowled. "How does that not make you angry?"

"Because I can't know for certain, can I? Besides, I didn't give up my magic. I just gave up my arm. The Grand Mage said if we gave up our arms, we would live magic-less lives, as though all our magic came from our ability to cast a spell. As though it's not a part of us, always."

Senna turned to the last drawing he'd done of her, stared at her rage and her sadness for a long time. "I didn't mean it, you know. All those things I said. Calling you a coward."

"I know." He knew, too, that this was her way of apologizing, and he hoped she could hear the forgiveness in his reply.

But then, to his surprise, she said it outright. "I'm sorry. I say things I don't mean because it's easier than letting you in. Letting you be nice to me. And I can apologize, but it doesn't make up for what I've said. What I've done. And I can't seem to stop myself from being this person I don't want to be."

"Maybe," he said softly, reaching for her hand, "you just have to keep trying. Maybe it takes practice."

"I don't think it's that simple."

"Nothing ever is. We all just try our best, again and again, until we get somewhere. Maybe all those mages who chose death couldn't realize that. I wish we could have shown them, convinced them they were more than an arm. But we're here. We're still here, and even if we never cast another spell, we've got magic. We can live a magical, beautiful, worthwhile life with art and flowers and fruit trees and dogs."

"And each other," Senna said. "You're my family, Lias. I love you." She laughed, a wild and beautiful sound. "That's me practicing being the person I want to be. Am I doing all right?"

"You're doing wonderful. I love you, too."

They were quiet after that, watching the rain taper off, holding hands while the dogs lay at their feet. Lias knew he'd draw it later, himself and Senna in the middle of the storm, this magic they'd created. Maybe he wouldn't be able to capture it all, but he'd try.

ABOUT VALERIE HUNTER

Valerie Hunter teaches high school English and has an MFA in writing for children and young adults from Vermont College of Fine Arts. Her stories have appeared in publications including Beneath Ceaseless Skies, Cicada, The Wax Paper, Colp, and Inaccurate Realities, as well as anthologies such as What Remains (Inked in Gray), Runs Like Clockwork (Wyldblood Press), Water: Selkies, Sirens, and Sea Monsters (Tyche Press), and Because That's Where Your Heart Is (Sans Press). You can find her on Instagram @somanystories_solittletime

ALL DEMONS GREAT AND SMALL

K.M. VEOHONGS

The first thing they did was steal my exclamation point.

Last night, when I saw the key missing from my laptop, I made excuses. These things happen. It means nothing. I must have knocked it off and not noticed.

I told myself other lies, too, as I got ready for bed. That the skittering of claws was squirrels on the roof, that the shadows on the edge of my vision were a trick of light. They weren't back.

But now it's morning and there's a weight heavy upon my chest. No use in lying to myself anymore. The loss of punctuation was only an opening salvo. The first shot fired in the latest battle in a war of decades.

I'm an old hand at this. I know their tactics. My shampoo will be buried, solid and unusable, in the back of the freezer. My clothes will develop persistent stains of unknown provenance. My shoes will go missing one by one until the only remaining pairs are painful or slovenly.

They're scrawny right now. Their tiny, hair-like spines are sparse and flaccid, their bellies sagging and empty. But it's only the beginning. Every day, they'll grow. Their spines will stiffen and burrow deep within my flesh. Their stomachs will swell as they feed on my doubt, my worry, my despondence. It will become a struggle to breathe as they gain mass and press their weight against my ribs.

Before my husband became of the ex variety, I would ask him for help. He never would. He tried — or claimed to. But when he called them off, it was half-hearted. The same manner in which he'd tell then-toddler Jason not to throw sand at the playground or kick me in the shins before going back to his book.

"Pull them off!" I would plead. "They're too heavy!"

He'd tell me he was late for work. "You're being dramatic. They aren't that big."

So, I learned to do it myself. It's better this way. It's better to solve my own problems and fight my own wars.

If only I could remember how.

The first step, I know, is to rise. It takes real effort to push away the dreams tainted by their overnight whispers, even more to shove their wrinkled bodies to the floor. But I do it because I have a son named Jason. (*But does he need you anymore?*) A job at First Mutual. (*You're replaceable.*) Friends named Lonnie and Megan (*who have their own families and their own problems*). I do it because the alternative is nothing.

I don't eat breakfast. They've broken all the eggs and spit in the milk, and one took a dump in the crisper. I rush out the door in an attempt to leave them behind, but they are sneaky, and I am not. They pile into the backseat, one lurking so close behind my left shoulder that I can smell its hot, sour breath.

At work I keep them in a cage under my desk. It doesn't silence their childish taunts. I am ashamed, not only because of how their words cut (*Ugly. Stupid. Useless.*) but by how affected I am by insults that wouldn't be clever in the mouth of a six-year-old. I try covering the cage with my jacket, but I can still hear them. I hit backspace again and again and again, repairing mistakes I shouldn't be making.

Megan comes for me at lunchtime. It's our ritual to go out on Wednesdays. Our special treat, we call it. It's my week to pick the restaurant. I was going to take her for Ethiopian, but suddenly

I'm sure she won't like it. She'll think it's weird, and that I'm dumb for suggesting it. But I cannot think of anywhere else to go.

Megan and her radiant smile appear at my office door precisely at noon. She notes the jacket-covered cage at my feet and her mouth fades into a frown. "You still haven't dealt with them?"

I insist that I *have* dealt with them, many times. It's only that they keep coming back.

"I've told you before. Walk them to the woods, chuck them into the underbrush, then run."

I think of my painful shin. One of them kicked me while I was getting out of the car. "I'm not sure that will work," I say.

A short huff of frustration. "How do you know if you won't even try? I know what I'm talking about. You've never seen mine again, have you?"

"No." I remember it though. There was only one, and it fit inside her pocket. "I did hear about an exterminator you can hire," I mention in a small voice. "To get rid of them? They put down a repellent, too, so it's harder for them to come back."

"You don't need an *exterminator*." Megan taps her foot and glances at her phone. "They aren't *that* bad. Besides, those people always pressure you into a maintenance plan. What a waste of money." She waves at my desk. "I'm guessing you can't go to lunch?"

One of them has gotten free and is changing all the numbers on my spreadsheet.

"No," I agree. "I can't go to lunch."

I stay late yet find myself more behind than when I arrived. I call Jason on my drive home. There was a missed call, but they deleted the number before I could check. It wasn't him, Jason tells me. He has an exam tomorrow. He can't talk. There's no point in trying Megan, after our canceled lunch. And if Megan hates me now, perhaps Lonnie does as well. Is there anyone else?

No. Probably not.

For dinner, I eat dry tortilla chips at the kitchen counter. I had went for the salsa, but the whole lot of them have piled up in front of the fridge. I tugged on the door, tried to nudge them away with my foot, but the largest bit my ankle, and I gave up. How did they get so big already?

A noise outside startles me. I wipe crumbs from my mouth with the back of my hand and move towards the slider to the backyard. *Intruder*, they hiss. *Burglar, rapist, murderer.*

A rare misstep. They've done their job so well that death might be a relief.

But never mind. It's only a cat.

She's rather small and very bedraggled. Mostly white, with one orange ear and one black. Her meow is loud for her size and audible through the glass. I raise a hand to the door handle.

Fleas. Mange. Rabies.

I hesitate as the cat's green eyes meet mine. She gives me a single, slow blink.

I open the door.

They creep forward, with snarls and gnashing teeth, ready to attack the small creature. I panic, not sure how or if I can intervene. What have I done? In my effort to help I have failed. I have condemned an innocent.

But, despite her tiny and tattered appearance, this cat is a fighter. She puffs out her coat to double her size and strikes. Having never been skilled at direct confrontation, they scatter into the shadows. The cat sits down and delicately licks a paw. After a moment, she lowers it and meows at me again.

The message is clear. I find a can of tuna. There's some in the pantry next to an unopened jar of salsa. We eat our snacks in peace, together.

My plan for the rest of the evening had been nothing. They attack me when I try to leave the house — pull my hair and nip at my heels. Easier to stay home. Or watch TV if they haven't yanked out all the cords. But the pet store is open until nine, and tuna is not a balanced diet for a cat. I take a deep breath, put my hand on the door to the garage, and brace myself for the assault.

The cat bolts forward and blocks their path to me. They fall back, glaring and whispering, but I can't hear the words over the cat's growling. They are now no bigger than she is and far more cowardly. I slip out to my car untouched.

In the morning, the weight on my chest has returned. I sigh as best I can, not wanting even to open my eyes to see them. Then a soft tap touches my cheek, and I realize this weight is warm. And vibrating.

I open my eyes.

Correction. The weight is purring.

The cat opens her mouth in a yawn, then blinks. Time for breakfast.

She doesn't let them follow me to work. Megan is pleased to see the cage empty. "You took them to the woods, didn't you? I told you it would work."

I nod and smile.

By the weekend, the cat has driven them outdoors. I can still see them lurking around the yard, but they're quite small. Just little dots of inky darkness spotting the grass. It's hard now to hear their taunts and whispers — they're drowned out by the sound of purring. I call Lonnie and tell her about the cat. She's happy for me.

Jason comes to visit on Saturday morning, although I had expected him the night before. He's carrying two full bags of laundry and is slow to close the door. I sigh when I see what has slipped in behind him.

Jason is introduced to the cat. She now wears a collar with a little bell and looks rather smart. Jason laughs at me, not unkindly (*unless it is*). "It's kind of a cliché, isn't it? The lonely single lady with the cat?"

I thought he would stay overnight. I was going to make waffles. But he tells me he has plans in the city and leaves once the last laundry load is dry and folded. "You may want to check lost and found," he says as a goodbye. "That cat might belong to someone else."

Two more slip in as he leaves.

They lure the cat into Jason's unused bedroom and shut the door. I pull on their arms and legs. I wail and kick at them, but they've somehow tripled in size in the last hour. I finally give up, weeping over the sound of the cat's distress. I fall onto my bed but cannot sleep with all their hissing whispers. The images they paint are vivid: a child weeping over a missing pet, my house overrun by cat hair and cat urine and cat feces.

The next morning I put the cat in the carrier. I try to cram them into the trunk, but they're too big. Instead, they pile into the backseat, reminding me that I work long hours, that vet bills get expensive, that cats eat their owners if left alone with their dead and cooling body. I try to shush them. I remind them that I'm doing what they want, but they won't shut up. I'm not sure which is worse: their hissing or the cat's mewling complaints from the carrier. I will silence the one I can.

I get to the shelter and carry the cat inside. *You're doing the right thing*, they promise. *Such a nice cat could never belong to you. She must have another owner.* The cat growls and thrusts one paw out of the carrier in a swatting motion. They fall back, one of their number wailing and bleeding. *We'll wait for you in the car.*

The woman at the desk is slouched and haggard. She turns, and I see she has one of her own, riding her back. She shakes it off with a grunt and kicks it into the corner. "Can I help you?"

But I've become distracted. There's a viewing window into the kennel area. A family crowds around the cage of a bouncy poodle mix, but the mournful dog next door is without visitors. His brown eyes are sad in the way of all lonely dogs, but I can't tell what color his fur is. He's covered in . . .

"What are those?" I ask the woman, pointing to the afflicted hound. "Oh," she says. "He came in with them. We used to pick them off each morning, but they always came back, and we just don't have the staffing."

"Are they permanent?"

She shrugs. "Maybe. Hard to say with an older dog like that. No one's been willing to take him home to find out. Can't really blame them." Hers is trying to climb up her leg. She shakes it off again and gestures at the carrier. "Are you surrendering?"

I look down at the carrier and then at the mournful dog. One hangs off a torn ear. I can barely see his face with how they cover him. There are so many. If the shelter can't handle them, why would I be able to?

The cat sticks her paw out again and taps my knee. Her gesture prompts another question: If I don't try, will anyone else?

"I'm not surrendering," I say to the shelter woman, and hers slides off her leg with a thud. "I came to adopt a dog. That dog."

The dog goes in the backseat, and the cat in her carrier takes the front. Them I corral into the trunk. They whine and gnash their teeth, but they fit just fine now, and I shut them tight within.

It takes hours. The dog is patient but large. His are different from mine: small and not very strong. But they are very, very stubborn and number in the hundreds. I have to detach each individual claw and tooth from the poor dog's abused flesh, stick them in the trash, then close the lid. Sometimes they bite me, but I don't mind. The wounds are tiny. The cat comes and goes, sometimes batting at one that tries to escape from the garbage, sometimes quietly grooming the dog's skin where the fur has been torn away. But even once they're all gone and sealed in the trash can with a roll of duct tape, the dog lies flat with his face pressed against the floorboards.

A wasted effort. I haven't helped at all.

The cat nudges my hand. It's time for bed. Maybe the dog will be better in the morning.

The cat warms the covers as I change into pajamas and brush my teeth. The dog slinks behind us into the bedroom, tail low, and drops to the rug with a heavy sigh.

That's when I hear the whispers. I had forgotten about them.

I thought they were still in the trunk. But now there are two, lurking by the bedroom doorway. They always come back.

But at the sight of them, the dog roars to life, leaping to his feet with a mighty snarl. They scream and run, the dog on them in hot pursuit. The cat's eyes go wide and I scoop her into my arms to join the chase. We find the dog in the kitchen, one already limp at his feet, the other trapped in his jaws as he shakes and shakes and shakes. Two more watch from the windows, but the cat hisses at them and they flee.

Once the dog is finished, I put on my coat and shoes and gather up their shrunken bodies. I decide that, perhaps, Megan's advice isn't entirely bad. The dog and cat both follow as I carry them to the woods behind my house, and dropkick them deep into the dead leaves and branches. The cat twines around my legs, and the dog wags a hopeful tail.

Before I have even turned back to my house, I see two of them peer at me from behind a tree. They are small, but they are relentless. They will not be defeated so readily. Not for long. I hustle the cat and dog back indoors and grab my purse. I know that's where I left it — the card for the exterminator. Lonnie gave it to me after my divorce. "There's nothing wrong with needing help," she had said ten long months ago. "They do good work."

I find the card and use a magnet to secure it to the refrigerator. I'll call them in the morning, but maybe I'll call Lonnie now. Just to tell her about the dog. Just to talk to someone.

A skittering sound freezes me in my spot. Already?

I make myself turn around. I can't get rid of them if I can't face them.

It's only the cat. She's found a bit of plastic to play with, batting it back and forth between her paws until it slides to a stop under my foot.

My exclamation point!

ABOUT K.M. VEOHONGS

K.M. Veohongs is a mixed race Thai-American writer living in New England with her family. Her alter ego is a veterinarian whose superpower is charming goats, and her work is featured in Translunar Traveler's Lounge and an anthology from Weird Little Worlds Press. She has a website at kmveohongs.com and you can also find her on Twitter @kmveohongs posting pictures of her pets and cheerfully complaining about writing.

IN TANDEM

KARL EL-KOURA

She couldn't see anything, but she wouldn't say that to her husband, who was next to her on his own v-bike. She had probably missed something simple, and the last thing she needed was to hear his exasperated explanation of how she'd failed to switch on the doohickey or whatsit on her visor before slipping it onto her head.

"It's all dark for me." Pete's voice came from beside her. "Do you see anything?"

"Nope," she said.

So curt, Pete thought. He knew that if these stupidly expensive exercise bikes were malfunctioning, he'd never hear the end of it. He'd declined the up-sell of in-home installation.

"I see something," his wife said suddenly, almost with child-like excitement. "Point your head to the bottom right. There's a question mark. It's a bit hard to see unless you're looking for it."

Sarah nodded in the direction of the faint symbol, and its hazy blue outline turned to a more intense white. "Welcome to Trainer World!"she heard from the speakers in the visor wrapped around her head. "I'm over here!"

She shifted her gaze and saw a small white blob-like creature waving a pudgy arm at her.

"Hello," she said sweetly. "What's your name?"

From beside her, she heard Pete say rudely, "And what are you supposed to be?" Her husband thought Sarah resented him for ordering these bikes on nothing more than a coworker's casual recommendation, but that wasn't true. He splurged on cool new tech toys just like she splurged on other things (as he'd once pointed out, out of the blue and unnecessarily, except perhaps to assuage his own buyer's remorse), but that wasn't the reason she couldn't muster enthusiasm for his new purchases.

They used to wake up an hour early every morning and go for walks around their neighborhood as the sun was just rising, but they'd skipped a day, then two. Then weeks went by. They used to play in a recreational volleyball league together, but work had gotten busy for both of them and they'd stopped that too. So when their counselor suggested they reconnect by picking a shared activity, Pete had ordered a pair of virtual reality exercise bikes. Pete's idea of a "shared activity" was something that allowed him to be in a world separate from her, just like most of his other cool new tech toys. *That*, not the amount of money he'd spent on the things, was what bothered her.

She focused on the virtual creature trying to get her attention.

"Sorry, little guy," she said. "Can you repeat that?"

The small round blob smiled and said, "You can ask me any question you have, any time you have it!"

"I don't see anything," Sarah said. "Except for you, I mean."

The blob looked around the dark world as if diagnosing the problem by sight. "Your v-bike is functioning properly," he said finally. "Have you started pedaling?"

Even though the blob was nothing but a computer program, Sarah felt her cheeks flush. Without removing the visor, she felt around with her feet for the toe cages and slipped them in. The straps tightened around her shoes, and she began to pedal slowly.

Just in front of her, a path of light faded in, and more wisps of light swirled into existence around her, which gave her the sense of movement as she began to travel along the path.

"Think of this world as a canvas you paint with your energy," the blob said, floating beside her. "Exercise every day and your world stays vibrant and rich; skip anything longer than one rest day and this world you create begins to fade away. Your energy sustains it, and it reflects everything you do. Your brain waves, your cadence, your heart rate, how long you pedal, what time of day you exercise — the world you create is unique because it uniquely reflects you."

Pete removed his visor and surveyed his wife. He didn't think she realized the sounds she made, how many wows she was saying per minute. He watched her now, bent over the bicycle and pumping her smooth legs. She'd looked very cute when she came down to the basement in her small black shorts and blue t-shirt, though he'd tried not to let her catch him looking. But now he let himself look at her, and he smiled at each expression of delight that escaped her lips. Those innocent exclamations, the unprocessed gut-level reactions to exciting or scary events in the world, were what made him fall in love with her in the first place. At that thought, though, he felt a pang of guilt and lowered his eyes. When the little blob-creature had detected another bike beside his and asked Pete if they were creating an individual or a shared world, Pete had immediately said individual. Now it occurred to him to wonder if Sarah had heard him make that choice. How would she have answered, he wondered, if she'd gotten the question first?

That night was Sarah's turn to cook. She had made shrimp and vegetable stir-fry with white rice while her husband sat at the kitchen table, scrolling aimlessly past news headlines and, she knew, almost randomly clicking on different articles to read.

After a long silence where the only sounds were made by their forks clanging against their plates, Pete looked at his wife and said, "So . . . what do you think of the bikes?"

"Incredible," Sarah said.

"Oh yeah?"

"A hundred percent. It's just . . . beautiful! Not the word I would've thought to use to describe an exercise bike, but it's the one that fits, isn't it? Mr. Blob was right. It's like a work of art."

"Mr. Blob?" Pete repeated then laughed.

"Can it go on forever, though?"

"Why not? It's like building a world. Mine's taking on a forest feel, lots of browns and greens, tall things all around. It's like a sketch of a forest right now, but I can see it taking more definite shape as I spend more time cycling. What does yours look like?"

Sarah raised her eyebrows and turned down her lips. She shrugged with her face, not her shoulders. "Looks like light, I guess? Lots of swirls of lights of different colors, but it's not really shaped like anything. Probably I'm not as disciplined as you. That's what my random pedaling has gotten me. Or maybe it's my random brain waves."

"Do you want to get on again after dinner?"

She didn't want to, because although they'd only used the bikes for less than an hour that afternoon, her butt and legs were already sore. Pete was the cyclist; she was a runner. But Pete sounded so excited — and lately it was so rare to get any emotion out of him that wasn't sadness or anger — that she nodded and was rewarded by a delighted smile.

The night before their appointment with Dr. Sadler, it occurred to Pete that he would have to sit on that stiff black leather couch and explain why he'd bought two stationary bikes that allowed each of them to escape into a world of their own.

Since they'd begun seeing her a year and a half before, his greatest fear had been that Dr. Sadler would lean back in her chair, peer at them through her small round glasses, nod her head as if some great enlightenment had come to her and say, "I'm going to be honest with you folks."

Was this going to be, finally, that moment of enlightenment?

"Try to sleep," Sarah mumbled from beside him. But she knew he never slept well on the night before their monthly appointment. Dr. Sadler had been her therapist before she'd agreed to take them on as a couple, and Pete had never really warmed up to her. And because Pete tossed and turned to work out his insomnia, Sarah never got much sleep either. So Dr. Sadler often saw the worst versions of themselves early on a Saturday morning after a night of restlessness, with one half of them wishing he were somewhere — anywhere —else.

Pete woke up before her and made the usual breakfast of bacon, scrambled eggs, and buttered toast. Once, Sarah had told him that she had loved waking up to the smell of frying bacon, and ever since then it had become tradition that he'd cook some up every Saturday.

She stumbled downstairs and sat at the kitchen table. Immediately, with the same fancy waiter's flourish he'd been using since they were first married seven years ago, Pete placed a mug of hot coffee in front of her, steam still rising in fading plumes.

They drove in silence to the parking lot of the tall brown-bricked building where Dr. Sadler kept her office. Silence up to the main entrance, where Pete stepped forward to open the door for his wife. It was instinct now, like making breakfast for her on Saturday mornings.

Silence too in the waiting room. He wondered how many couples sat quietly in a therapist's office and how many carried on a conversation and whether the difference was a predictor of therapeutic success. If he were a marriage counselor, he decided, he would install a camera in his waiting room and then tell the couple right away if they had a chance or not.

"You okay?" Sarah said.

"Fine," he said, without looking at her.

Sarah kept staring at him. *He resents me for dragging him here, month after month. Resents waking up early on Saturdays, resents the cost, resents having to open our marriage to* — what was that word that she'd had to discreetly look up afterward? — *a vivisec-*

tionist. And yet, here he was, wasn't he? Despite not liking Dr. Sadler and absolutely hating her black leather couch, despite all his grumbling, he went with her to the appointments *every time*. And, she had to admit, though never to him, he was especially handsome when he moped.

Dr. Sadler came into the waiting room, and with a small wave of a hand invited them into her office.

"How have you been?" she said when they'd all taken their seats.

The couple sat next to each other on the couch, but weren't touching. In the first few sessions, Pete had made a point of sitting very close and often had held her hand in his. But that was a show he put on for Dr. Sadler and, after a while, he'd given up the effort.

Usually Pete let Sarah answer first, but this time he responded right away, almost blurting out the words like a confession. "We got exercise bikes. We've been using them almost every day."

Dr. Sadler's warm but mostly neutral smile stretched out into something more excited. "Exercise bikes! Really? Well, that's wonderful."

"They're virtual reality ones," Sarah said without looking at Pete. "So we don't really talk when we're using them."

"I wasn't thinking about that when I bought them," Pete said. "I just thought they'd be . . . cool," he ended lamely.

"They are pretty cool," Dr. Sadler said. "My husband and I use them at the gym in our building."

Pete seemed to relax for the first time that morning, leaning back into the squeaky leather. He kept his posture neutral, but Sarah could tell it was taking a lot of effort for him not to seek her reaction to this revelation.

"They're great little machines," Dr. Sadler said, "but not exactly what I had in mind when I said you should try to exercise together. Let me repeat something I said earlier, but I'm going to be a little clearer and a lot more prescriptive, all right? Pete, Sarah needs time every day to just talk to you. Not about anything in particular, just about her day and your day and anything else that comes to mind. Sarah, Pete needs to be doing something, accomplishing something. That's why I suggested a shared activity. Pete, how long are your riding sessions when you use the bikes?"

Pete looked at Sarah. "About an hour?"

She nodded.

"Alright," Dr. Sadler said. "Then I'm telling you to spend at least half the time on the bikes not wearing the visors at all. So thirty minutes with visors, then take them off but keep pedaling. Sarah, that's your time to talk about anything you like or, if you want, not talk at all." Dr. Sadler leaned back in her chair. "I want you to try something else for me, too. My husband and I tried this and really enjoyed it. I want you to switch visors."

"Put on each other's visors, you mean?" Pete said hesitantly, as if she'd just suggested they try on each other's underwear.

"That's right, Pete. The world is stored in the visor, so put on your wife's so you can cycle through the world she created."

"Dr. Sadler," Pete said, still very unsure, "that feels a bit . . . violating. And it would change the world she's created."

"What do you think, Sarah? Would that be something you're comfortable with?"

"Sure," Sarah said.

"Pete, how about you?"

Pete couldn't say *no* now that his wife had already said *yes*. He decided on: "I suppose we could try it?"

Sarah placed her hand on Pete's leg and patted it lightly, her way of signaling to him that she wouldn't hold him to it.

That evening, although it was Sarah's turn to make dinner, he offered to help and they worked together in the kitchen, measuring and chopping and mixing and, yes, chatting.

Because she appreciated the effort, at dinner she said, "We don't have to switch visors."

"You don't want to?" he said.

"I know you don't."

Pete hated when Sarah tried to read his mind, not because she was wrong — since almost always she was right — but because it didn't allow him any room to do anything for her. It was easier to acknowledge she was correct — never in words of course — and follow along the path she set out for them. But he'd been doing that for the last, what . . . *two, three years?* and it wasn't working.

He rolled a small piece of naan, dipped it in his bowl of butter chicken and said, "It makes me a little uncomfortable. But I am very curious about the world you made. A world of light; I'd like to see that for myself. And I guess it's only fair to show you mine." He smiled boyishly and popped the small sandwich into his mouth.

Sarah ignored the performance and said, "If you'd really like to, we can."

"Sure. How about this . . . we'll go downstairs once we're done with dinner and whoever created the best world does the cleaning up?"

"You've turned this into a competition," Sarah said, leaning over in the chair as if falling off. "I think I may die of shock." She paused for effect, then straightened with her own winning smile, which Pete seemed to appreciate as much as she'd appreciated his. "And how will we know which world is the best one?"

"We'll know," Pete said.

"Fine with me," she said. "It's too bad. I would've helped you with clean up."

She regretted the words as soon as she put on Pete's visor. They hadn't even bothered to change into their workout clothes or shoes. They went right down to the basement and mounted their bikes. Then, as if exchanging something as solemn and personal as wedding rings, each had removed their visor from its charging stand on the handlebars and handed it to the other. Pete had put on her visor right away.

She watched him for a minute, curious to see his reaction to her world, but it was impossible to read with half his face obscured behind the shiny plastic arc encircling his head. She slipped on his visor.

The view always faded from black as one pedaled, as if booting up or kick-starting the world's sun, probably because they'd discovered that was less disorientating. And as Sarah began to pedal, Pete's world appeared, a world of tall trees reaching up to a beautiful blue sky, of hanging long green leaves, of gently flowing rivers, of wooden bridges over streams that somehow gave her the sensation of being rocked when she cycled over them. A tiny bird, something like a hummingbird with feathers of bright blue, flew down from one of the overgrown trees and flapped its wings at her as if challenging her to a race, then spun around gracefully and darted off. She chased the little thing for a while, until her burning legs and lungs insisted she concede defeat.

It's a real world, she thought, half in awe and half in despair. *Not like mine; mine's a weird abstract thing of colored lights criss-crossing each other.* She felt embarrassed that she had gotten to cycle Pete's beautiful rainforest and, in exchange, had let him into her weird maze of navigable lasers.

She stopped pedaling and removed the visor. Pete wasn't on his bike. With a pang of sadness that quickly turned to anger, she thought that he could've at least pretended to enjoy it to spare her feelings. At least wait for her to finish, find something nice to say.

Upstairs, she found Pete standing at the kitchen sink.

"What are you doing?" she said.

"Dishes."

"Pete, stop." She placed a hand on his back. He finished rinsing off the dinner plate, then placed it in the drying rack before turning around. He had a strange expression on his face, something she couldn't interpret. Was he doing this out of guilt for not being able to stand her world for longer than a few minutes?

"I'll clean up," she said, trying to gently move him out of the way. Pete didn't budge.

Again, Pete thought, *it'd be so easy to go along with you. To leave you with the dishes if that's what you want, and I can go off and do my own thing.* But, instead, he decided to say what he was thinking. "Nope. A bet's a bet, Sarah. And my world sucked compared to yours."

Sarah searched his face for evidence that he was making fun of her. But that was a momentary fear, because she knew Pete well enough.

"I liked your world," she said, quietly. "It's wonderful."

"That's nice of you," he said. The look on his face was that mopey hangdog she found kind of irresistible. "But let's be real. My world is a forest. You can find forests all over the planet. Your world . . . I've never seen anything like it. Cycling along those paths, going upside down? Riding horizontally? It was breathtaking. You said you had random brainwaves, but riding through your world made me feel like my brainwaves are boring and pragmatic and that yours . . . well, yours are creative and brilliant."

"So why did you stop?"

"I didn't want to mess up your world."

"But that's silly," she said. "I don't care about that."

Pete took a deep breath. "Listen, I know Dr. Sadler said we need to pedal and talk —"

"We don't have to."

"No, we can. We will, okay? But I have another idea if you want to try it tonight."

"What is it?"

He took her by the hand and led her back downstairs, then waited for her to slip on her visor before putting on his. He activated the cartoonish white figure they'd named Mr. Blob, although the name was less fitting the more they used the bikes.

"How can I assist you?" Mr. Blob said.

Pete said, "Do you detect the bike beside mine?"

"Yes. Would you like to create a shared world?"

"Yes," Pete said. "Don't erase the world she's created, but I'd like to create a new one with her."

"Please hold," Mr. Blob said.

In Sarah's view, what she understood to be Pete's Blob appeared and asked her if she was okay creating a shared world.

She couldn't help but think that Pete's blob was better defined than hers had become.

"Sure," she said.

Pete reached out with his hand until he found his wife's and squeezed it.

Together, slowly at first, they began to pedal.

ABOUT KARL EL-KOURA

Karl El-Koura lives with his family in Canada's capital city, holds a second-degree black belt in Okinawan Goju Ryu karate, and works a regular job in daylight while writing fiction at night. Visit www.ootersplace.com to learn more about his work, and find him on Twitter @KarlElKoura.

THE STARLING

LINDSAY MANSFIELD

She stares at her mother's body in the bathtub. Her face is pale, lipstick astray.

Death-stained water spills onto the floor. The cat, not concerned with getting wet, laps at the creeping crimson.

Cadence remains frozen in the doorway, disconnected from a reality she can never return to.

Footsteps echo along the hallway. They come to a stop behind her.

"What the —"

He pushes past. Her stance falters, but she remains in place, frozen.

"Jesus Christ! What the fuck have you done!"

He — Porter, father — kneels in the bloodied water next to the bathtub. He takes his wife's limp hand in his, checking for a pulse, but there is nothing. He drops it. It thuds limply against the bathtub. He shakes the blood from his hand in disgust and grabs the radio from his belt as he wipes the remaining death onto his trousers. They are already ruined. One more stain won't make a difference.

"Tom? It's Porter. Can you send someone to 349 Marshall Street?"

A static pause lingers.

"349 Marshall Street? Isn't that your house?"

Frozen. Dead.

"Yeah, yeah it is. Circe — the damn bitch has gone and killed herself. Can you get a clean-up crew here pronto? The cat's making a real mess of itself in here."

Cadence stands alone in front of her mother's grave dressed in a black coat. The red ribbon she tied around the daisies is too tight. Now their white heads flail on broken necks, coming to rest against her cold hands like velvet tears.

The small group behind her share their condolences with Porter, but not with her. She is invisible. The only person who ever saw her is now dead.

Five people mill around Porter, who is dressed in his uniform. He is always dressed in his uniform. Deputy Tom stands stoic by his side while an older couple over-sympathetically coo at the tragic loss: "So young, so beautiful, taken too soon." Blah, blah, blah. A scantily clad blonde woman rests a hand tenderly upon Porter's arm while the Priest tries to avert his eyes from her blooming cleavage.

Cadence places the broken posy upon her mother's grave. The headstone reads:

CIRCE PORTER

1994-2021

There is no epitaph.

Laughter erupts from the small group. It is only when she hears her father laughing that she comes to realize he never even cried.

Cadence had only seen her mother cry once. She would often hear her crying through blistered walls after the yelling and screaming had stopped and Porter had left. But she had only seen her cry once, standing by the kitchen sink, staring blindly out the window.

Cadence had asked her mother, "Mama, what's wrong?" to which she replied, "Nothing, baby. It's nothing," while wiping away the tears with the back of her hand. "It's just the onions."

There were no onions.

A shrill chipping breaks Cadence from her reverie. She follows the sound to find a small bird under a tree: a starling, feathered but not yet a fledgling. Its beak opens wide as it calls hungrily for its mother, but Cadence sees no other birds. She reaches down and scoops up the tiny creature. It panics. She gently strokes its tiny head with her thumb.

"Have you lost your mama?"

The shrill chirps of the bird dissolve into squeaks and trills as it calms within the warmth of her hands.

"I've lost my mama too."

The small bird closes its eyes.

Cadence opens her coat pocket and carefully places the bird inside. It panics once more in the absence of her touch. She cups her hand to the outside of her pocket and the trills trickle into silence.

"Shh," she soothes. "It's okay. Everything is going to be okay."

Cadence looks at the starling. It sits upon her bed inside a shoebox lined with tissues, opening and closing its beak as it silently begs for food.

"Have you lost your voice? Probably just as well. You're a noisy little thing."

She reaches into the box to pet the bird, but the bird thinks her finger is a worm and tries to eat it.

"You must be hungry. What do you even eat?"

Porter is still dressed in his uniform. He always wears his uniform. He is snoring on the couch with the cat curled up asleep next to him. The only light comes from the pornographic glow of the laptop that sits on the coffee table next to the overflowing ashtray, surrounded by crushed empty beer cans.

Cadence tiptoes into the living room and makes her way towards the computer, careful not to wake her father. Porter snorts and groans but continues to sleep. The cat, however, is now awake. It watches Cadence intently as she kneels before the laptop. Paying no attention to the video on the screen, she closes the window and opens a fresh browser page. In the search bar she types: WHAT DO BABY STARLINGS EAT?

"I hope it tastes better than it smells."

Cadence dangles a soggy cat kibble from a pair of tweezers. She feeds it to the starling who gobbles it up eagerly. A quiet warble escapes from the bird.

"Shh . . . Dad can't know you're here."

The bird cocks its head to look at her, as if it understands her plea.

She feeds the starling more kibble until it has had its fill. It hops onto her hand.

"You really need a name."

Cadence looks around her room until her eyes fall upon the photo sitting on her bedside table of her mother. *Circe.* A mythological enchantress with the power to transform others into animals. If only her mother had been able to transform, then maybe, *just maybe . . .*

"Circe. I will name you Circe."

The mornings are a blur of strange women, stale breakfast cereal, cigarettes, and burnt coffee. Every morning Porter thumbs out three fifty-dollar bills from his wallet and throws them down on the table. He leaves without saying a single word. Cadence is always invisible — always, except for today.

"Shouldn't you be at school? It's been like, what? Four weeks?"

The scantily clad blonde from the funeral sits across from her. Out of all the women Porter has bought home, she is the one he likes to fuck the most.

Cadence doesn't look up from her cereal. "Two and a half."

"What?"

"Two and a half. It's been two and a half weeks."

The blonde reaches into her bag for a cigarette. She flicks and grinds the lighter five times before the flame sparks to life. "Still. You should be in school."

"It's Sunday."

"Yeah, well, what about Sunday school? You know, Jesus and all that crap."

"I don't believe in God."

The blonde woman takes a long drag of her cigarette. She taps the ash, but it misses the ashtray and lands on the table. The blonde doesn't notice. She exhales coils of smoke.

"I wonder if she believed in God. You know, before she —"

The blonde woman makes a cutting motion with her finger along her inner forearm, her cherry red fingernails like razors. *Inhale. Exhale.* Wild smoke shimmering, writhing in the light. "Stupid bitch," she mutters. "Why the fuck would you kill yourself?"

Cadence snaps her head to look at the woman, hair falling from her face in ringlets to reveal dark bruising around her left eye. Her rage is a current. *Because of this!* Cadence wishes she could say. *She killed herself because of this!* But she remains silent, wishing to once again become invisible.

The cat claws and mews at Cadence's door. She shoos it away and enters her room alone. It is breakfast time for Circe. Cadence reaches under her bed for the shoebox. The lid is gone, and the shoebox is empty. Her stomach plunges.

"Circe? Circe! Where are you? Circe?"

She hears a familiar chirp. Cadence looks up to see Circe sitting on top of the curtain rail.

"How'd you get up there? Did you fly?"

Circe chirps again before fluttering down to land on Cadence's shoulder. The small bird nuzzles into her hair affectionately and trills with content. Cadence takes Circe from her shoulder, and the bird perches on her finger as she sits down upon her bed.

"I wish I could fly."

Cadence looks towards her window, fearful that she is beginning to understand what it was her mother would blindly stare at whilst pretending not to cry. Nothing. The sweet freedom of nothing.

"Then I could fly away from here."

Circe looks at Cadence inquisitively.

"Of course, I'd take you with me. You are all I have left."

Porter and Cadence sit at the dining table. Sunday night is the one night where Porter insists that they all sit down at the table like a proper family for a proper meal. Except they are not a proper family. They had never been a proper family.

Anticipation hangs in the air, like swirling ozone before a storm. Cadence does not like this feeling. She pushes food around her plate absently with her fork.

"Amber-Lee thinks you should go back to school."

Cadence doesn't bother to look up. She stares at her plate in the same way she stares at her cereal bowl in the morning: trying to ignore the ever-changing parade of women and their breakfast of cigarettes and cask wine.

"And which one is that? The brunette with the short hair? Or the one with the tongue piercing? Oh wait, that was Candy. Or is it —"

Porter's chair gouges the vinyl as he rages from his seat, hand ready to strike. Cadence looks up at her father, but all he sees is her already blacked eye. He sits back down with a huff, straightens his Sheriff's badge, and brushes imagined creases from his shirt. He always wears his uniform. Porter clears his throat and continues.

"Amber-Lee was here this morning."

"Oh, you mean the blonde."

Porter swallows hard against his anger and tries to retain his composure.

"Yes. The Blonde." He takes a sip of his beer. "Amber-Lee and I think it's time for you to go back to school. Now I know it's a Sunday, but I ran into Ms. Clements today and —"

"You and Amber-Lee think what?"

"I *ran* into Ms. Clements today and said you would be in class tomorrow."

"But it's too soon!"

"You *will* be going back to school tomorrow. The bus will be here at eight, and I expect you to be on it!"

Cadence pushes herself up from the table, sending her chair crashing to the ground. She runs towards her bedroom.

"I hate you! I wish you died instead!"

Cadence's alarm goes off at 7:00 AM. It startles Circe who had been sleeping in the now lidless shoebox on the bedside table. The bird starts to chirp, trying to mimic the *warmp warmp warmp* of the alarm.

"Shh, Circe, quiet . . ."

Cadence turns off the alarm, and Circe stops chirping. She gets out of bed. Her freshly-pressed school uniform hangs from the handle of her wardrobe. It was the one thing her father knew how to do well: press uniforms until they resembled crisp army attire. She looks at the small bird and sighs.

"I'm sorry, but I have to do this alone."

Cadence stands in front of the bathroom mirror brushing her teeth. She can see the bathtub in the reflection. The clean-up crew had been unable to remove the bloodstains. They tried industrial grade cleaners, hydrogen peroxide, and even vinegar. They scrubbed and scrubbed and scrubbed, but nothing could remove the stains of her mother's death.

Cadence is dressed in her school uniform with her hair tied neatly back into a ponytail. She had thought of leaving her hair out to obscure her now yellowing black eye, but Cadence knew she could only hide it for so long. It was better to face the devil. As she leans forward to spit the toothpaste out, she hears a loud crash, followed by the sound of breaking glass and a banshee scream.

"Circe!"

Cadence runs from the bathroom, down the hallway, and skids into her bedroom. Her mother's photo lies smashed on the ground next to Circe's empty box.

Circe is sitting on the curtain railing, screeching frantically as the cat tries to climb the sun-faded linen.

"Cat! No! Get away from her!"

Porter bursts into the room behind her, startling the cat who runs out puffy-tailed and hissing.

"What the hell is going on in here?"

He sees the bird perched upon the railing. Its shrill screech thrums in his ears.

"Where the fuck did that thing come from?"

Porter does not wait for an answer. Even if he did, it would make no difference.

He draws his gun.

Cadence screams.

Porter aims.

Porter fires.

BANG! BANG! BANG!

The first bullet shatters the window, clearing the way for the second. The third slams into the wall, sending plaster fragments and shrapnel flying. Circe falls to the floor.

"No! Circe!"

Cadence pushes past Porter. His stance does not falter. She scoops up Circe's lifeless body.

"Circe?" chokes Porter. It is the first time he has spoken his wife's name since he radioed in her death.

Cadence turns and faces her father, holding Circe's limp and bloodied body up for him to see.

"You! You did this! And you're the reason why Mama's dead! I wish you were dead! I wish it had been you in that bathtub!"

She pushes past Porter and runs out of the room.

Porter, still stunned by the sound of his dead wife's name, remains. Frozen in silence.

Cadence runs out the front door, along the path, past her father's patrol car, and down the street. She runs towards the cemetery. She runs towards her mother.

Cadence collapses upon her mother's grave, acid in her blood and tears. The wilted remains of the white daisies lay at the base of her headstone, still bound together by the too-tight red ribbon. Cadence places the body of the small bird on top of the dead flowers. Circe's blood matches the ribbon and stains the flowers red to match.

"Why does everything I love have to die?"

A patrol car pulls up alongside the cemetery gates. Porter, dressed in his uniform — he is always dressed in his uniform — gets out and strides towards his daughter.

"You know you can't just up and leave like that!"

He reaches the grave of his dead wife and grabs Cadence by her ponytail, dragging her to her feet.

"You don't think I miss her? I miss her every goddamn day! You ungrateful little shit. You're the one who should be dead! Not her, not me, you!"

Cadence kicks and flails, fighting with all her might. "No, no! Let me go!"

Porter spins her around. Cadence squeezes her eyes shut and waits for the blow to come.

There is silence. Her mother stands by the kitchen sink, staring blindly out the window. *Nothing, baby. It's nothing.* She should have never looked for the truth in her mother's eyes. She should have looked for it within her own heart.

The blow does not come.

Something behind Cadence catches Porter's attention.

The morning sky above the cemetery darkens and begins to move. Thousands of small shapes twist and turn amidst the shadows, swooping and swirling together in a hypnotic aerial dance.

Hundreds – *no, thousands* – of starlings descend upon the cemetery, the murmuration choreographed to sharp precision.

Porter watches the spectacle with confusion and trepidation.

"I thought they only did this at dusk?"

He lets Cadence go. She cautiously steps away from him and watches the sky.

Without warning, the flock descends upon Porter. He waves his arms frantically to shoo them away.

"What the fuck? Fucking birds! No. No, No!"

His cries turn to screams as the birds swarm him in a thick fog of feathers and claws and beaks and cries. Cadence watches on in silent awe and horror.

Porters' screams diminish into a whimper, then from a whimper into silence.

The murmuration subsides as quickly as it formed until there is not a single bird in sight. All that remains of Porter is his badge.

Uncertain of what exactly she has witnessed, Cadence walks hesitantly towards the badge. Shaking, she reaches down to pick it up, but is interrupted by a familiar chirp.

She turns to see her starling, her Circe, perched atop her mother's headstone, alive and unharmed.

Cadence walks towards Circe with her arm extended. Circe flies towards her and lands on her hand. Cadence gently pats the small bird's head. Circe trills with affection.

"Come, let's fly away from here."

ABOUT LINDSAY MANSFIELD

Lindsay Mansfield writes horror and speculative fiction - or whatever has captured her attention for the month. When she is not writing, she can be found yelling (loudly) at video games. Lindsey can be found on her website, lindsaymansfield.com or on Twitter @L_A_Mansfield

OF FRIENDS AND FLOATING ORBS

MATT BLISS

Gregory Carmichael finally lassoed the orb on his thirteenth try. The rope slipped around its glassy black surface until he pulled the loop tight with a firm tug. It wobbled in its place, still hovering above Gregory with the rope hanging from it like a thin tail.

"There," he said, placing hands on hips and grinning up at his catch. He wrapped the cord around his hand and leaned against it. Almost improbably, the orb moved. Still keeping its distance from the ground, trailing behind like a dog out on a walk, just like the day they all arrived.

Greg let out a satisfied shriek. He led the object along the freshly trimmed grass, out to where his bike waited patiently in the street. Slender hands worked loops around the chrome rack, and after checking twice that it wouldn't fall off or get stuck in his spokes, Greg straddled the bike.

Gregory braced himself on the bicycle, feet on pedals, hands flexing against the handlebar's grips, eyes narrowed down the strip of blacktop laced between rows of pastel houses. He pushed off with a sudden jerk, heaving against the pedals until the orb gave a hesitant lurch and a wobble, and fell in sync with the bicycle.

Gregory craned his head, watching it follow his winding path, blotting out the sun as it passed this way and that. He laughed just loud enough to hear it above the clicking sprocket and the wind howling in his ears. *Who needed a kite*, he thought, *when you could have one of these?* He watched the other orbs lining the street as he passed. They didn't move, and Greg wondered if they ever would.

Before Gregory knew it, he was facing the cedar fence at the end of the street, stomping on the brake, and skidding to a halt. The orb, however, kept moving. It passed overhead and pulled at the bike with enough force to knock Gregory to the street. It drifted a moment still, scraping his cherry red bike along the asphalt as it ground to a stop.

Still lying there on the pavement, Greg stared up at the dark sphere above him and cheered. Despite the scraped knee and scuffed up bike, he was free. Free like he never had been before. No more living in fear. No more hysteria. Now, it was only Greg and the life he had made.

"You shouldn't do that, you know," said a voice from behind him.

Greg turned back to see a girl standing above him. She had one eyebrow cocked as if she had been waiting her whole life to say something, do something like this.

Greg stood and brushed dirt from his jeans. "Shouldn't do what?" he asked, staring straight into her dark walnut eyes.

"Play with them. My mom won't even let me get near them."

Greg swatted a hand at the air between them and, pressing a flat hand to his forehead for shade, looked up at the orb.

"You don't even know what they are. No one does . . ." The girl tramped into the street and pressed herself between Greg and the orb. "My mom says this is how it starts." She leaned close and whispered, "The invasion."

"Invasion?" Greg turned the other way and propped up his bike. "Please . . . they don't do anything except float there. If they were going to do something, they would've done it by now."

"You don't know that. No one knows. The smartest people on Earth haven't figured it out, what makes you so sure?"

"Well, maybe I know something they don't."

"Oh yeah?" She folded her arms over her chest. "And what's that?"

"Well." Greg tugged on the rope and watched his orb wobble above him. "Maybe they just need a friend."

The girl huffed from her nose. "Or maybe *you* need a friend."

Greg swelled at the words, lifting a chin toward her and straightening his spine. "Maybe I do."

Suddenly, the girl's posture changed, and the smallest of dimples formed in her right cheek.

"I was going to take it down to the creek. You want to come with me?"

She paused a moment and finally gave a resolute nod. "But not on *that* thing," she said, pointing to the bike. "I've seen how you ride it. I'd rather walk."

"Okay then." Greg snapped down the kickstand. "We'll walk."

The girl fell in step with Greg as he casually led the orb through a sunlit afternoon toward the copse of trees at the end of the road.

"I'm Jessie," the girl said as she bounced along. There was a slight skip in every one of her steps. "And you're Greg, right? I've seen you before, at school. Back when we used to go."

The orb let out a faint hiss. A sound not unlike the rustling of trees. Greg looked up and squinted, but saw nothing different.

The two walked, staring at their feet until concrete turned to damp grass. Gregory passed the line of birch trees, needling the orb around branches of yellowing leaves until finally stopping at the creek's edge.

"It's beautiful," Jessie said as Greg tied the rope around a tall, gray boulder. She squatted at the water's edge, pressing a finger into the glassy surface. "I've never been here before."

Greg sat next to her. "Sometimes I like fishing here. Sometimes I just lie in the grass and listen to bugs. Forget about every-thing going on out there."

Jessie flopped back and let out a long breath.

Greg moved next to her and did the same.

The orb clicked then, shifting ever so slightly closer, pulling the rope taught against the boulder.

"So if you don't think it's an invasion," Jessie said, raising a finger to the orb floating above, "why do you think they're here? Why don't they, you know . . . *do* anything?"

Greg turned to face her, propping himself on an elbow. "Well, I think it's kind of like this." He plucked a flat rock from the ground between them and held it flat in his hand.

"A rock?"

"Yeah. It's just a rock, right? But if I give it to you, and you take it home, leave it on the side of your bed or a windowsill — somewhere special — suddenly it's not a rock anymore. Every time you looked at it, you would remember the person who gave it to you. And when you held it and closed your eyes and thought real hard, just *maybe* you can still smell the creek from the day you got it. The way it felt in your hand. The heat of it . . . It's all there, but it isn't. You know?"

Jessie took the stone from his hand and ran a thumb over its surface.

"It's a reminder," Greg said, easing himself back down and staring up at the orb with cheeks pinched back into a smile. "A reminder of what else is out there. That we're not as alone as we think we are sometimes."

Jessie held the stone to her chest and lay back in the grass. "I like that," she said, and angled herself over until the top of her head touched Greg's. "I like that a lot."

The orb hissed again, twisting in its place and swelling. It blotted out the sun, casting them in shadow. And there, in that darkness, wasn't the orb, but a vast stretch of stars. A swirl of lights spinning around a galaxy of brilliant violet. The creek was gone, and now they were among the stars, riding the ring of some faraway planet. When Jessie reached out and locked a pinkie around Greg's, suddenly anything seemed possible.

The two woke up with a start and sat up among the fireflies dancing below a darkening sky.

"I must have nodded off," Jessie said, still clenching the stone in her hand. "It's almost dark. I better get home."

Greg blinked the haze from his eyes and rose up to help her. "Me too, I'm sure. I'll walk you home." He moved to untie the rope holding the orb to the boulder, but cocked his head sideways, noticing it was already undone.

The orb moved easier, it seemed, as they weaved through the trees and returned to the row of pastel houses with street lights twinkling like birthday candles.

Jessie stopped in front of her house. "Thank you, by the way. I had fun." She held out her hand with the rock resting on her palm. "I want you to have it."

Greg laughed as he took the rock. "Thanks."

"You can put it on your windowsill, and every time you see it, you'll have to think of me." Even in the dark, Greg could see her dimple.

Someone called Jessie's name, and she quickly darted inside.

Greg found his bike, kicked up the kickstand, and walked home. "Thank you," he said, turning up at the orb. "For the best day of my life."

He returned the orb to the side of his house where he had found it and moved to tie the rope to his fence, but paused. Instead, he let it hang free. He looked up at the glassy black surface, running his thumb over the rock, still smelling the creek and damp earth it came from. "A reminder," he said, tossing the rock up, catching it, and placing it in his pocket. And as he walked away, feeling less alone than when the day had started, he swore he heard the orb say something, but it probably was just the wind rustling through the trees.

ABOUT MATT BLISS

Matt Bliss is a construction worker turned speculative fiction writer from Las Vegas, Nevada. He believes there's no such thing as too much coffee and is the proud owner of too many pets. His short fiction has appeared in Metastellar, Cosmic Horror Monthly, and other magazines and anthologies. If you don't find him haunting the used book aisle of your local thrift store, you can always find him on Twitter at @MattJBliss.

THE CHOCOLATE FAIRY

SARINA DORIE

My first-grade teacher told the class that people who keep their desk clean were visited by a special kind of fairy godmother — the chocolate fairy. From an early age, I had a healthy appetite for all things chocolate, so it was no surprise that this sparked my interest.

"She's related to the Tooth Fairy and Santa Claus," Mrs. Fritz said.

"Santa isn't real," Jeremy Peterson said.

I rolled my eyes. Everyone knew you couldn't believe anything Jeremy said. Besides, I had caught a glimpse of Santa once, so I knew he was wrong.

Mrs. Fritz smiled in her benevolent way. "The chocolate fairy doesn't care if you believe. The only thing she cares about is a clean desk. She leaves gifts to those she deems worthy."

I looked to the cubbyhole in my desk crammed with tissues as rough as sandpaper that were smeared with boogers, broken crayon nubs that had fallen out of the box, and half-finished extra credit worksheets in disarray. School supplies had spilled from my pink pencil pouch. My desk was one of the more egregious messes in the classroom. I never felt like I could keep up with other first graders. It was one of those childhood inadequacies that had started once I'd realized I was adopted.

Even before I'd known, when I played outside with other children, I'd never had the sense that I fit in. Perhaps that strange sensation of chaos building in my life was really caused by untidiness. The one thing that seemed to relieve that pressure — that longing — was chocolate.

I wanted — no, needed — the chocolate fairy to visit me. After I finished my math worksheet, I cleaned out my desk.

The following day I found a mini Snickers in my clean cubbyhole. My mouth watered.

The chocolate fairy had noticed my efforts! From that day forward, I was trained like Pavlov's dog. The chocolate fairy didn't always come to my desk, but when she did, she brought the good candies: Mounds, Twix, Kit Kats, and Milky Ways. After each little reward, I felt as though I was about to float away like a hot air balloon filled with pure joy.

That was the best year of my elementary school life.

Possibly the most hyper as well.

Twenty years later, my employer at the advertising agency called me into his office and sat me down. "Saoirse, we need to have a talk about . . ."

I leaned forward in anxious anticipation. One of the graphic designers had been fired last week. Was I about to be laid off? It wasn't like I enjoyed my boss's long rambling speeches at meetings, the numerous occasions he didn't pay employees on time, or how often he allowed clients to change their minds on the scope of advertisements after I'd already started, but it was a job. I needed some kind of income.

He cleared his throat. "It's your desk."

That was why he'd called me in? "What about it?"

"It's a pigsty."

I stared at him, my mouth agape. "It is clean. It's just untidy."

He crossed his arms. "It's unprofessional. I want it organized before you leave."

I trudged out to my desk, humiliated that I was the Pigpen of the office. Two of my annoying coworkers nudged each other and giggled as I passed them. Of course they had perfectly immaculate desks. I felt as out of place here as I had in my first-grade classroom. These people had never struggled with a disorganized day in their lives. They didn't know what chaos was like and how hard it was to keep it in control. Weren't artists supposed to be messy?

I supposed I should have been thankful I hadn't been fired, and I'd been given this opportunity to correct my behavior. If I cleaned my desk and I blended in with everyone else, my boss would be less likely to fire me if he cut more positions. Yet, it was hard to be grateful for a position earning a salary just above minimum wage when every day I felt as though a little more of my soul was dying.

I felt like Cinderella cleaning my desk, annoying coworkers peeking at me from their cubicles like wicked stepsisters. As I brought order to my workspace, my resentment eased away. I forgot about my ego and what other people thought of me.

Cleaning my desk was cathartic, as if I were removing a diseased limb from a tree. Some of the ache in my soul lessened. Yet as I gazed out the skyscraper at the cluttered city where I lived, I didn't feel like I had done enough. I wanted the entire world to feel as clean and free as my desk. It was a strange craving. I waved it off.

After work, I told my husband why I'd arrived home late.

"Now that you mention it, your mess has taken over this desk too," he said, waving a hand at the shared desk in the corner of the living room. "Maybe you should tidy up the one here."

Tears filled my eyes. He obviously didn't understand what I was going through after being humiliated at work. He didn't understand that irrational alienation I had felt my whole life.

He must have misunderstood because he said, "It's easy. All you have to do is make sure it's clean every day."

"I didn't ask for advice," I said. This was just like Randy, telling me how to fix something instead of listening and saying, "That sounds rough." That was all I wanted to hear.

I cleaned the plates of mostly finished food hidden under newspapers, sandwiched between sedimentary layers of folders, bills, and printouts. It was true my bad habits had taken over at home too, and it wasn't fair Randy was forced to share in my mess.

A little more of the tension in my soul eased once that desk was clean too. I felt oddly satisfied, like I used to in Mrs. Fritz's class after tidying my cubbyhole.

In bed that night, I told my husband about the time I'd been visited by the chocolate fairy.

Randy laughed. "That's brilliant! I bet that would have gotten me to clean my room as a kid. We should do that for our kids. When we have kids, I mean."

"What do you mean by 'do that'?" I rolled over toward him. "Do what?"

"We should give our kids chocolate to bribe them to clean their rooms. It's a great idea for a teacher to reward students with positive reinforcement, but they might not have someone giving rewards at school that way. We should do it here for them."

"But if we do that, the chocolate fairy — or fairies — would be out of work." I thought of the people at work being laid off. "They would lose their jobs and have to try to make ends meet on unemployment."

My husband propped himself up on one elbow. "You're hilarious." He kissed me on the cheek like he usually did to say goodnight.

"Also, Mrs. Fritz told us most people aren't ever going to be visited by the chocolate fairy. Not everyone is up to her standards. And she doesn't visit all the time. Also, only special people will ever see the chocolate fairy in action. Mrs. Fritz saw the fairy once when she was a kid and told us all about it." Enthusiasm bubbled out of me as I remembered my teacher's tale.

"Um . . . so, was that her parents dressing up or something?" Randy asked.

"No! It was the chocolate fairy." I had stayed up late numerous times to try to see her but never had.

"Oh, uh-huh." Randy was oddly silent. "Good night."

In the morning I found a Lindor truffle on my desk at home. At work, it didn't completely surprise me to find the chocolate fairy had done double duty. She had visited my office as well. I had been gifted with dark chocolate salted caramels. The chocolate fairy had definitely scaled up the chocolate gifts since I'd been seven.

At home that night, I cleaned my sewing machine table. The following day, I found a small Godiva bar. The chocolate fairy had renewed my love affair with cacao — and cleaning. I strove to keep my desk at home and the one at work tidy. Serenity filled me as I embraced this orderly and well-kept side of myself. Occasionally I was rewarded for my extra efforts with my favorite candies.

Always chocolate. It was heaven for my soul.

The day after my husband cleaned his messy leather working counter in the toolshed, he brought a Clark Bar into the living room office and waved it in front of me. "Are you trying to sabotage my keto diet?"

I stared at his favorite candy, my mouth watering. "No. Why do you ask?"

He scowled at me. "You left this on my bench. I'm not eating chocolate. Jerky, pepperoni, and cheese are my rewards now."

I threw up my hands in exasperation. "The chocolate fairy doesn't know that." I doubted the fairy knew what to do with an all-meat diet.

"I know it was you. Stop acting like it wasn't." He dropped the bar into the garbage.

"It wasn't me!" I didn't know why he had to be like that.

When he wasn't looking, I dug the bar out of the garbage. A

Clark Bar wasn't *my* favorite, but I wasn't about to waste good chocolate.

I understood the chocolate fairy didn't have a treat for a person like Randy, and everyone deserved to be rewarded for their cleanliness. And perhaps, just as importantly, I wanted to help the chocolate fairy too. I had loved her ever since she'd left a present in my desk as a child. I did research on the Internet and ordered a package of stevia-sweetened, dark chocolate-covered bacon.

Using my creativity this way felt far more satisfying than designing packages, arranging stock art on websites, or selecting color schemes for apps. Something in my soul awakened in the act of playing chocolate fairy. I felt alive again.

The keto-friendly chocolate arrived two days later. I set the package between the rows of neatly arranged tools on my husband's workbench for him to find.

That night in the kitchen, Randy snuggled up behind me and kissed me. "That was a nice treat. Was that for cleaning? Thank you!"

"It wasn't me. It was the chocolate fairy." I couldn't meet his gaze. Oddly, I felt guilty, like I was taking work from the chocolate fairy.

The following night, I was up late working from home on an advertising project that had been thrust upon me. The scent of chocolate wafted into the room. I closed my eyes and inhaled. The air tingled with happy feelings that reminded me of my childhood.

The sound of foil crinkled, and I looked away from the computer to find a balding old man with a magic wand that resembled a chocolate-covered pretzel rod flashing psychedelic colors. His wings glowed green.

The chocolate fairy wasn't small or female. He defied everything I'd imagined. Except the iridescent dragonfly wings. They were everything I had imagined a fairy would possess.

"Oh my!" He regarded me over a pair of wire spectacles.

"You're the chocolate fairy!" I gasped.

"Indeed." He tilted his head to the side, studying me like I was the unusual one. "How peculiar. You can see me?"

I nodded emphatically.

"I suppose there's no real harm in it." He lowered his voice conspiratorially and winked. "Just don't tell anyone you've seen me. I'm supposed to be a secret."

I felt like a child again, filled with wonder and awe at the magic of the world. The magic of chocolate. I remembered that glimpse of Santa I'd gotten once. "Like Santa and the Easter Bunny?"

"Not precisely. Santa Industries is more of a corporate title. And the Easter Bunny — well, never mind." He waved a wand over my desk. A small package of chocolate-covered cherries appeared next to my keyboard.

"Thank you!" I hugged the box to my chest.

"No! Thank you!" He smiled in a kind and grandfatherly way. "You have been doing a fantastic job keeping your desk clean and helping restore balance to the universe."

"What?" My eyebrows shot up in surprise. "Is that what happens when people keep clean desks?"

"Pretty much. It's an important duty, and someone has to do it."

I had always felt like the world was overwhelming and full of chaos when I let the messes in my life get out of hand. Apparently, it hadn't been my imagination.

The chocolate fairy backed away as if about to exit, then hesitated. "I heard about the little mishap earlier with your husband. And no, I can't give away my source." He coughed, and it sounded like he said, "Bogeyman."

He waved his pretzel wand toward the garage. "Sorry about the confusion with the Clark Bar and the keto thing. I can never quite keep track of these fad diets. I'm just not as young and savvy as I used to be." He grinned, his face wrinkling up. "I'm grateful that you corrected my error."

"No problem. I'm just glad you aren't mad. I didn't

want to insult you." If I was a chocolate fairy, I would put my skills with spreadsheets to good use keeping track of people's chocolate preferences, dietary restrictions, and allergies.

"Not at all. It's rare anyone uses chocolate as positive reinforcement these days. Except schoolteachers and parents potty training their children." He raised his wand, looking like he was about to leave again.

"Wait!" I swallowed the sudden lump in my throat. I didn't want the chocolate fairy to go. I didn't want this moment to end and to return to my normal, chocolate-free life.

"Are there any openings for chocolate fairy positions?" I held my breath, afraid he would look down at me with disdain like my boss did.

"It's funny that you mention that." He chewed on the chocolate end of his pretzel wand. "I've been wanting to retire for over a century now, but I'm the only chocolate fairy left to carry on the tradition."

"Why aren't there any other chocolate fairies?" Maybe the job didn't pay well or his boss was a jerk.

"All the other fairies are drawn to more exciting jobs like cupidry, being a fairy godmother, or they join Santa Industries. And the thing about this job, you have to really love chocolate."

"I do!" I said. And I couldn't imagine anything more exciting than this job. Santa was highly overrated.

He folded his wings behind him as if he intended to stay longer. "A fairy has to be able to sense chaos in the world created by humans and their slovenly ways, though that's a minor detail. Some of that skill can be developed with on-the-job training. A fairy has to . . ." His eyes flitted behind me to where my wings would be if I were a fairy.

A lump of dread dropped into my belly. I understood. "I'm not a fairy. I don't have wings, and I can't use magic." All I had was an Amazon account and a credit card.

Never before had I ever felt so heartbroken.

He pointed to my package of chocolate-covered cherries with his wand. "Have a bite of chocolate."

I considered arguing that chocolate wasn't going to make me feel better, but that would have been a lie. Chocolate always made me feel better. The moment the bittersweet cacao touched my tongue, the tightness I hadn't realized was constricting my chest released. I breathed easier.

He nodded decisively. "Close your eyes. Imagine how light and free you feel. So buoyant that you could float away."

I followed his instructions. I did feel light and carefree.

"Imagine flapping your wings to fly," he said.

I noticed he didn't say, "Imagine what it *would be like* to have wings."

I had no doubt in my mind I had wings. Air rushed against my cheeks as I flapped iridescent wings with venation similar to his, though mine were shaped more like a bumble bee's.

I opened my eyes when something tapped my head. I floated above the office area of the living room, my head touching the ceiling. Turquoise light radiated from me.

I could fly! I glanced over my shoulder to find my wings flapping. I tilted, off-kilter, and somehow managed to smack myself in the face with a wing.

I let out a squeal of startled surprise and dropped toward the computer chair. The chocolate fairy aimed his wand at me and my descent slowed so that I landed onto the chair with an "Oof."

Wings I hadn't known I'd possessed bumped into the chair.

He chuckled. "Obviously you need lessons."

"What does this mean? Am I a fairy?" I asked.

"Indeed. It's quite extraordinary. A fairy living among humans." His eyes were full of sympathy. "You must have felt so . . . out of place here."

I nodded emphatically, tears filling my eyes.

He smiled. "You need a mentor. I think you'd do well with a change of career paths."

"When can I start?" I was so ready to quit my job at the advertising company. Being a chocolate fairy sounded too good to be true. "But this is a real job, right? I will get paid?"

"Indeed. Fairies have a system for these sorts of things." He held up a stern finger in warning. "I should warn you, though, as a chocolate fairy you will be required to keep fastidious records and meticulous organization. And your desk must be . . . immaculate."

I glanced at my own desk, which was in a state of perfection at the moment. Papers were neatly stacked in trays, garbage and recycling had been properly sorted, and I'd returned pens, paperclips, and sticky notes to the drawer. Not that it would stay that way without an incentive. "Can I give myself chocolate for keeping my own desk clean?"

"Every day!"

I was so on board with this!

That was how I got my new job as a chocolate fairy. Every day I get to reward people for restoring balance to the universe.

ABOUT SARINA DORIE

Sarina Dorie has sold over 200 short stories to markets like Analog, Daily Science Fiction, Fantasy Magazine, and F & SF. She has over eighty books up on Amazon, including her bestselling series, Womby's School for Wayward Witches.

A few of her favorite things include: gluten-free brownies (not necessarily glutton-free), Star Trek, steampunk, fairies, Severus Snape, and Mr. Darcy.

You can find Sarina on her website, sarinadorie.com, or on Twitter @SarinaDorie

SEEING TURQUOISE

ARWEN SPICER

Bibi looked out the big, new window and started to cry. In the distance, the mountains were a postcard-perfect blue. Try as she might to keep her eyes there, she never could for long. Inevitably, they drifted down. There was no not looking.

She turned away and thawed a mouse for Barleycorn.

"Here you go, little nipper. Yes, *I know*." Her pet fenkin weaved around her legs, purring loudly and tail bushed. With a snap he was in the corner with his prize.

Bibi ground some imported sovo beans for her breakfast malt. It took more time than grabbing a Likwid Lunch from the fridge, but it was rest day, so she took it slow. Her back still to the window, she swung onto a kitchen bench.

"Screen, morning news, please."

The screen descended from the ceiling, state of the art. She hadn't wanted it, couldn't afford it, but all the new house models came with them. The news came up, live and amidst an interview segment: an older man chatted with a younger guy.

"*It's just something about people, isn't it?*" said the older. "*It's like on the one side there's saving the biosphere and on the other there's a Brisky's double helping of spareribs. And it's like biosphere or Brisky's? Biosphere. Brisky's. And it's like, 'Yeah, I'm taking the Brisky's.'"*

The younger man laughed. *"Exactly. It's like 'I can imagine the end of the planet before I can imagine life without spareribs.' But so then, how do we cut consumption?"*

"Well, the answer is basically we're screwed."

More laughter.

"Screen, off, please."

Bibi took her malt and went outside. The spring morning felt like the turn of summer, the grass poking through cracked earth was half yellow, the oats gone to seed a full month early. The feather breath of spring wildflowers had given way to the sturdier blooms of the dry months. In some patches, the grass had never even started, autumn leaves still brown on the dirt. A bluehead vulture wheeled off behind a neighboring hill. At least they were doing all right. Must be lots of dead things to eat since the fire.

She tried not to look down the hill at the corpses, but still they insisted on catching her eye. Half the elia forest had died in the blaze, leaving her hilltop bald and baking. Five years on, the skeletal trees had lost most of their thinner branches, and the stumps of their limbs poked weirdly up, like damned souls reaching out in supplication . . .

"Stop it, B. Stop it!" she told herself.

But she couldn't unsee it. Why today? She woke up to this hilltop every day. Why was it hitting her like this now?

She sat on the porch step and sipped her malt, letting the tears roll. When she closed her eyes, she could still see the lush spring of her childhood: butterflies ducking among the blooms, the branches of centuries' old elias spreading over her, eternal.

When she first came home after the fire, she wept for the loss. Yet, suspended for a moment, that eternity persisted. In those early days, most of the dead trees still stood, like iron sculptures leafed in gold beneath the blazing blue of the autumn sky, immortalized as if by some prodigious metalsmith for the garden of an emperor. She'd looked up from the blackened earth, and all the world was blue and golden.

An irony lay buried in that blue-gold harmony.

Everyone here was a Golden now, at least partly. Bibi herself showed no trace of any other racial ancestry. Her hair was gold, eyes a golden brown. She would like to claim that she belonged to the only home she'd ever lived in, but everything about her said *colonist*, the child of invaders.

The soap weed.

That's why it was hitting her. Because yesterday in class, she'd done the soap with the kids, "just like the Turquoise used to make it." But the truth was, she didn't know how they'd made it. The kids never came out with decent soap, and Bibi's own was scarcely better. Book instructions. She had no clue, yet bizarrely it was the best she could do for the school's unit on the Turquoise.

Absurd.

It's not *people* eating spareribs while the world dries. It's Goldens. It's us. Only Goldens are like that. But we're not the whole damn world, or we didn't used to be. The Turquoise lived here for thousands of years with no problem.

But they were gone now. Oh, there were still tribes around the country. But here in Mill Run, on Vulture Turquoise land, they were all gone. *The only people who could tell us how to live here without killing this place, and we killed them.* That's what that book in the college library had said.

And then a new thought occurred. She'd read that book years ago, before the whole world went digital. Just that one book. What if it was wrong?

She went inside.

"Screen, bring up Scribble, please."

The screen melted into the face of a Golden woman with a wide, fake smile. "What can I help you find today?"

"A history of the Vulture Turquoise people in Mill Run, up to the present day."

"Oral or written output?"

"Written, please."

"Certainly."

The screen dissolved into an article titled "Indigenous Peoples of Mill Run, Uestaria."

She stepped up to the screen and adjusted the size, then swiped through it, tapping links: history of Mill Run, history of the Vulture Turquoise. The last time a Vulture Turquoise tribal member had recorded in the census was seventy-seven years ago. Gone, just like the book had said.

Bibi went back outside into the rising heat. A chainsaw blared at the Makeggors' place. Closer, there came a vigorous knocking, followed by the squawk of a woodpecker. They'd hit the jackpot since the fire: dead wood everywhere, teaming with beetles.

Barleycorn was snuffling at the woodpile that used to be Momo, the huge elia she'd climbed as a child. She didn't know what to do with the wood. Grandpa would have burned it in the fireplace, but fireplaces were illegal in these new houses due to the fire risk.

Weird that Grandpa hadn't had any books about the Turquoise. He'd had a reference book for every occasion: encyclopedias, dictionaries, bird guides, plant guides, history books — but not about the Turquoise, as if they didn't matter.

She knew what he'd say, though. "Go back to the library, B. If we don't have it, look wider. Never mind these newfangled digital doodads. You never know what you'll find in the stacks."

The Mill Run Public Library was open on rest day till mid-afternoon. It was small but had some quaint local archives. You never knew. It was two miles from her house, five minutes' drive, but that felt like a sin — the energy consumption, pollution for nothing. It was a nice day, a slow day.

"Come on, Barley. We're going for a walk."

Not far down the once-wooded road, Barleycorn started yipping and yanked at his leash.

"Not so fast, nipper. What you see? . . . Oh."

It was a pigeon perched in a dead elia, some weird little goggles strapped to its head, almost like reading glasses.

"You okay, sweetie?" Bibi called to it. "You somebody's pet — or a carrier pigeon?"

As she stepped forward for a better look, Barley lunged. The leash slipped from her hand. He made a leap at the pigeon, and it took off.

"Barley! Come!" she cried as he sped after it. She thundered into the yellowing grass. "Barley, no!" With a wild skid, she caught the leash and held him, not twenty feet from the fence with the sign: *Posted, No Trespassing. Keep Out.*

It was a sore spot for her, the Makeggors' land. When she was five, it had been her magic kingdom. She could still picture those three towering spurs of rock, her castle guarded by a single spreading elia. A year later, the Makeggor's built their house and she wasn't allowed there anymore. She hadn't seen it in thirty years. She made a face at the sign and headed for town.

On Elia Street, the elias were gutted, stumps or stragglers sprouting broccoli balls out of burnt-black limbs. The neighborhood was an expanse of denuded lots, half-vacant, half-rebuilt with big monstrosity houses and attempts at green in the form of over irrigated bushes. It was becoming a desert town.

Down by the bistro, it wasn't so sad. The fire had missed the downtown, and the cobbled square bustled much as ever. A scruffy young man in glasses strummed a guitar for a handful of listeners. The green tint to his hair said Turquoise blood — or that he had dyed his hair. He sang out with gusto.

Just 'round the corner,

Just up the street,
There's a world that's a-waitin'
To relieve us from the heat.

I wish, thought Bibi. It was easy to sing about the Big Dry, harder to get people to give up their Brisky's. Still, she respected him for trying. As she tossed a few coins in the hat, he gave her a funny sideways nod, almost like he was gesturing back toward her house.

Barelycorn snuffled his sandal.

"Don't be rude, Barley." She pulled him away as the guy's voice trailed behind her . . .

Just back up the road there,
Just past the sign . . .

The printout on the darkened door read:

Barley tugged at his leash again. He was scrabbling to get around the corner of the building.

"Dang it, what is your beef today? You looking for the water bowl? Bet it's empty." But she indulged him in taking a turn into the parking lot.

A solitary sedan was parked there, trunk open, an old lady grappling to get a big box of books inside it.

"Ma'am, let me help you!" Bibi hurried toward her, slipping Barley's leash around her wrist.

"Thanks, honey. I've got it. I've just . . . just got . . ." The top book hit the asphalt with a thwack. "Oh damn."

Bibi picked it up.

"Bless you, sweetheart." The old lady stuck the box in the trunk and wiped her forehead, making no move to claim the book.

"Library's closed, isn't it?" said Bibi.

"'Fraid so. I'm just here to pick up the recycling."

"Recycling? Not resale?"

"Not likely." The lady picked a book from the box and peered at it, wire-rimmed glasses perched low on her nose. "*Dinner Etiquette for Young Misses*, not a hot seller."

Bibi glanced at the book she had picked up: water-damaged, the title almost illegible. *Vanity*? No, *Valley*. *Vulture Valley*. *Vulture Valley . . . Tours*. A travel book? She cracked the cover. No title page. She started reading.

"Now way back when, there was a big storm that scattered all the flying people, and Gray Head Vulture, who was Dull Beak Vulture's nephew, got separated from the grownups . . .

She glanced at the cover and read it right this time. "Could I keep this?"

"Huh? Oh sure. It's worth less than nothing."

Barleycorn pranced around the Bibi's legs, doing his food dance. "Okay, nipper, hold on. Where's that treat?" She rifled through her pockets and delivered it to him. "Ma'am, thank you so much . . ."

When she looked up, the sedan was gone. She glanced out at the street. No sign of it. How could she have been that distracted?

A little shaken, Bibi started for home, then decided to pick up some lunch at Freshie's. It meant extra landfill — but biosphere, bubble tea? Biosphere? Bubble tea?

Sitting down with her tea, she gave Barley half her sandwich and started to read.

Gray Head Vulture went searching all over the land for his family, down in arroyos and up bluewood forests — half of the bluewoods had burned by now. After a long time, he saw some people — Vultures — circling in the air above . . .

Bibi leaned forward in her chair.

. . . a peak shaped like three arrowheads, like a father arrowhead with two sons by his side, and the mother elia watching . . .

It was the Makeggors'. Her childhood castle. She read on hungrily.

Gray Head Vulture met up with his people, but he'd been gone so long he'd forgotten who he was. "Tell me the story of who I am," he said.

His uncle replied . . .

Her eyes ran down the words, but she was no longer reading. *I've got to go there*, she thought.

She couldn't explain it, but it felt like she'd been summoned.

Leaving Barley at home, Bibi picked her way toward the Makeggors' yard, the same grass she'd pounded through that morning, but now, in the throb of afternoon, it had a different nature. Cicadas ratcheted, drawing life from the heat. The gold and purple summer flowers sprang up in profusion. It surprised her to see butterflies among them, even a few large tiger-tails. The surviving elias were in bloom, spreading yellow tassels of pollen in the breeze.

With only the slightest hesitation, Bibi passed the *No Tres-passing* sign, ducking through the old wire fence. She made her way up a hill specked with pink flowers in stubby, browned grass. Strange yet familiar. Quiet as a deer she went, intensely aware of the Makeggors' house, just out of sight around that slope. I she turned the other way and went around that other bend — yes, she could see it now, the pinnacle of her castle, the father arrow, and beneath it —

She froze.

There was a woman there, too young to be Mrs. Makeggor, heavyset with a bright green ponytail, gazing up at the dead elia — and then, crap, she'd seen her.

"You know this is private property," said the woman.

"I — is it?"

The woman smiled. "It's posted everywhere."

"Is it? I, uh, just thought . . ." Bibi was stumped.

The woman waved her over. "Don't sweat it. It's not like I'm the owner." She took something out of the bag at her feet and tossed it toward the foot of the tree. A vulture hopped down and snatched it. "These are rescues." She gestured at the three gray-headed juveniles craning their necks at her greedily. "Someone found them in their nest, half-starved. Orphaned probably."

"You do wildlife rescue?"

"Yeah, as part of habitat restoration."

She took a dead rat from her bag and held it out to Bibi. "Want to help feed them?"

"Sure." Bibi took the rat.

"Seriously?"

She tossed the rat in the direction of the vultures. "My fenkin eats mice."

The woman chuckled.

"You come out here often?" asked Bibi.

"Yeah, most afternoons."

"And Mrs. Makeggor hasn't caught you?"

"Caught me? Old Ms. M.? She *wants* the land restored."

Old No Trespassing herself, thought Bibi. Imagine that. Imagine being *allowed* to visit her magic kingdom again. "You think . . . I'd be interested in helping out."

"If you can commit some time," said the woman. "We're always looking for volunteers."

"You're with an organization?"

"Water Watchers — it's a tribal thing. But we take non-tribal volunteers."

A tribal thing?

Bibi's heart did a leap. Just like that, there'd been a tribe all along and somehow the books — the Goldens' books — forgot about it?

"I didn't know there was a Turquoise group around here," she said, trying to sound casual.

"We're not officially recognized. We're pretty small and kind of, well, mixed up, honestly."

"Mixed up?"

"You know, forgot a lot. Trying to piece together who we are, pass it on before our elders pass."

"I'd love to learn!" said Bibi.

The woman gave her a startled look. "Oh . . . well . . ."

Together they watched the vulture tear at rats, the sudden silence firm between them.

I got it wrong, thought Bibi. Too fast, too pushy. My people have taken everything from her people, and here's me asking for more. That wasn't what Bibi wanted, just taking and taking. She wanted to give back. But she was just a stupid Golden. *She* knew nothing, she had nothing to give.

The vultures fed, the woman gave her an awkward grin. "Well. See you around." She slung her bag on her shoulder and started off toward the road, leaving Bibi with a sense that she was vanishing forever.

If only Bibi had something . . .

All at once, the book weighed heavily in her purse. But it was hers. It had come to her like magic. It might be her only way to learn.

The woman was almost out of sight in the trees.

Bibi ran after her. "Oh hey."

The woman looked back.

"This is a weird coincidence, but I just picked up this book at a library giveaway." She fished it out of her purse. "It's on the Vulture Turquoise. I don't know, you probably already know everything that's in it, but if you'd like to see it . . ."

The woman took the book and paged through it slowly. "Damn, this is some old anthropological batshit."

Was it? Just more colonial crap? "Sorry."

"No, I didn't mean it like that. There might actually be some useful stuff here. We're always looking for . . . bits, you know? Anything, anything from before."

"Please keep it."

"You sure? Thanks." The woman tucked it into her bag and smiled.

Back at home, the sun blazed down out of a blue sky so perfect no artist could paint it. Tiny white butterflies fluttered among the flowers, and a breeze off the distant ocean made waves of gold in the grass.

Barleycorn's pointy noise peeked from the living room window.

Wrung out and open wide, Bibi drank in the living air. She had her hand on the door latch when she saw the business card wedged in. The logo was two eyes with reading glasses, no name, no contact, just a message scrawled on the back in blue pen:

Some things aren't in books but right there if you look.

ABOUT ARWEN SPICER

Arwen Spicer is a science fiction writer from Sonoma Mountain, California and has a scholarly background in Utopia Studies. Following the burning of her home in 2017, she has explored climate grief in both fiction and non-fiction. Her recent fiction has been published in the Ursula K Le Guin-inspired collection, Dispatches from Anarres, and Fabled Collective's Women of the Woods. Arwen lives in Portland, Oregon with her partner, two very teenage teenagers, and their feline household deity. You may also find Arwen through her blog (labingi.dreamwidth.org).